Martha Reynolds

For Leah —
with lots
of love,
Martha

VILLA DEL SOL

ISBN-13: 978-1977819628

ISBN-10: 1977819621

for J.L.

Death can release a person from a desperate existence.
Unknown Author

CHAPTER ONE

My husband died in the early hours of Christmas Day. He drifted away from life as I slept alone in our bed. I did not hold his hand or whisper words of love as he lost consciousness. I did not witness his final breaths, I did not feel for a pulse. Instead, his trusted doctor left me to sleep and woke me just after pronouncing Jonathan dead.

Jonathan's state funeral was a dignified event attended by thousands of loyal constituents. Even Vice President Guzman was there, and spoke at length about the senator's 'dedication to everyone, no matter their standing in life.' Mourners lined the streets; some waved small American flags as our limousine passed. The funeral was televised by the local media and was fed as a ten-second clip to the national news. I stood behind his flag-draped coffin at the cemetery and watched as it was lowered into the ground.

On the eighteenth day after I buried my husband, I sat in the airport and waited to board. The first time I flew on an airplane, I was a 26-year-old newlywed. The second time I was a 34-year-old widow. I was mindful of time passages. Eight years — how long we were married. Thirty-seven years — the difference in our ages. Eighteen days since his casket was lowered into the cold earth, twenty days since he lay in the State House Rotunda, and three weeks after he took his last breath of air.

I had a sleeping pill for the flight, which I fingered in my pocket. Sleep had eluded me for the past few weeks, and my doctor had written a prescription, but only for three pills. The other two were packed in my suitcase, nestled in the belly of the plane.

It was January, and unseasonably warm for New England. The house we had lived in together for nearly nine years, the house he had shared with his first wife, where they had raised their daughter, was mine now. I left it in the hands of my realtor, who had leased it to a professor at Brown University. The house was within walking distance to the campus, was spacious, clean, furnished, and ready to move in. I no longer wanted to live there.

I touched the pill once more and looked at my watch, anxious to board. I closed my eyes and tried to form a mental image of somewhere peaceful, anywhere else. There was Jonathan, and he was smiling. We were on our honeymoon in Puerto Rico, when everything was still new and exciting. I could see it all for a moment, but the picture faded away.

Finally, we boarded and I secured my seatbelt. The seat next to me remained empty, and the flight looked to be only about half-full. I didn't want to have to talk with anyone, anyway, and had armed myself with a book. I listened as the flight attendant spoke, and shook my head no when offered headphones.

The plane lifted off and I shivered at the momentary weightless feeling. Flying involved a great level of trust.

A male flight attendant who looked enough like Bradley Cooper to make me stare offered a choice of chicken or 'the vegetarian option.' He spoke in crisp, lightly-accented English.

"It doesn't matter," I said. I pulled down my tray table, even though I didn't think my stomach could handle a meal.

"Miss? You choose," he nudged. His pale blue eyes locked onto mine for an instant before I looked away.

"Chicken is fine, thank you," I said.

"And to drink?" It sounded like 'trink.' I wouldn't have any wine, not if I was going to take the sleeping pill.

"Just water," I said, forcing brief eye contact. A lot of people thought I was a bitch, an ice princess. That's what they wrote about me in the newspapers, that's what

I read online. I never admitted to it, but I did read the comments people posted online. I read them all. The newspaper cut me some slack after Jonathan died, but the comments section of the online story…people were vicious. The worst offenders posted their comments under an alias. 'JavaJoe.' 'OnePatriot.' 'HateLibs.' One woman, 'Anna4America,' suggested I had killed my husband. 'We all know Jennifer Logan was the ultimate gold digger,' she wrote. Seventeen thumbs up, two thumbs down.

"Bubbles or still?" His succinct voice interrupted my thoughts. I looked up to see him holding a quart-sized bottle in each hand.

"No bubbles, please." He placed a plastic cup of water on my tray table, then rolled away to serve the next customer.

I had little appetite, but figured I should eat something. When was the last time I'd eaten? I couldn't remember. The past two weeks were blurry and forgettable. My assistant Nancy, my *former* assistant Nancy, who helped me to secure the rental, was the only person I trusted. As soon as everyone knew about Jonathan's death, it was as if I no longer existed. The governor and his wife didn't like me, I knew that. They'd been close friends with Jonathan and his first wife, and they no doubt viewed me as most of the people in the state viewed me, as the self-serving trophy wife of the senior senator from the great state of Rhode Island. No one blamed Jonathan for marrying a woman who was younger than his daughter. They loved him, no matter what.

I left my tray dinner untouched but drank plenty of water. The pill remained in my pocket throughout the flight. I tried to read but couldn't concentrate. I tried to sleep but my mind wouldn't settle down, and by the time we were an hour from landing, I had no need of the sleeping pill. Bradley Cooper returned to me with another tray.

"Perhaps you eat breakfast, miss?" He winked. "And just before we land, I will bring you chocolate."

"I won't say no to chocolate," I replied, accepting a cup of hot coffee. He set another plate on my tray table. A roll, a wedge of cheese, sliced apple, yogurt. I sipped the coffee and looked out the tiny window. The landscape below was white. It may have been warm at home, but it was still winter, especially in Europe.

**

Nancy, who had traveled extensively throughout Europe with her husband, had directed me to a woman named Sarah, who ran a vacation rental agency in the Swiss capital of Bern.

"Sarah is wonderful, Jennifer. My husband and I have used her agency — remember when we took that three-week trip to Geneva and Mont Blanc?" I did remember. "Everything will be fine," Nancy had assured me with a motherly pat on my arm. Nancy was like that, motherly. I had no one to compare her to, certainly not my own mother.

With her help, and with Nancy's suggestions, I booked a six-month lease of a villa in the southernmost part of Switzerland, a place that, I was promised, was quiet and unassuming. Sarah and I had a telephone conversation the day before I left Rhode Island.

"I will send one of my employees to meet you at the airport, Mrs. Logan. Today I am not certain which employee it will be, but he or she will hold a large card with your name on it, so please not to worry. You will be escorted to the villa."

"How long will it take to get there?" I'd asked.

"From the airport, a little more than two hours. Our trains are very efficient."

Stuck on a train for hours with a total stranger had caused me some trepidation. It was precisely what I wanted to avoid, and exactly why I had chosen to travel to a foreign country.

The airplane bumped down on the runway and braked hard. A few people in the plane clapped when we stopped, applauding the pilot for not crashing us. I stayed seated until everyone else had deplaned, then stood, took my carry-on bag from its overhead compartment, and made my way to the exit. Bradley Cooper stood at the opening, thanking the passengers for flying with him. As I approached, he turned his pale blue eyes to me.

"It was a pleasure to serve you, miss. Welcome to Switzerland."

"Thank you. I hope I'm in the right place." I didn't realize I'd said it until it was out. It wasn't like me at all.

"Yes, customs to the left," he said as I walked away.

I slid my passport under a glass window. A uniformed man without expression took it, flipped it open, glanced up at me with keen eyes. I held his gaze, emotionless. He stamped my passport and slid it back under the window.

"Welcome to Switzerland," he said in a voice devoid of any accent and hand-signaled for the person behind me to step forward. I moved out of the way, tightened my grip on my bag, and followed the signs to baggage claim.

A six-month stay would require enough clothes to

see me through a change of seasons, but I packed minimally. Whatever I needed, I was sure I could find. It was far more important for me to just leave.

I waited in front of a large carousel with dozens of other weary travelers from my flight. Most of them stared down at their phones. I was glad to have arrived without one. One objective of my journey was to disconnect, and I had decided to unplug for the duration of my stay. Nancy was incredulous when I'd told her. No cell phone, no email, no internet, I'd declared. I was adamant.

"But how will you stay in touch?"

"Stay in touch with whom? You'll know how to find me. You have the address and telephone number for the villa, you know Sarah at the agency. There's no one else who will need to find me," I added with a wry smile. No one cared. And I wasn't being dramatic. They cared about Jonathan. Maybe they had an interest in what my financial windfall would be, but I'd be long gone by the time any of the nosy reporters might find out. They hated me, and I…well, I didn't hate anyone. But I didn't like them, that was for certain. And I could leave them all behind. My mother was in a safe place, and cared for. She didn't need me. She didn't even recognize me.

"I'll really miss you, Jen," Nancy had said when she

dropped me off at the bus station. "I wish you'd let me drive you to Boston. Or I would have called a car for you. You don't need to ride on the bus, you know."

I knew very well. But for the first leg of my trip, it was what I wanted. Enough of being the senator's wife. Riding a bus from Providence to Logan Airport was more me than anyone could have guessed.

"I'll miss you, too, Nance. I'll send a postcard, and you know how to reach me if it's important. But nothing should be important. Besides, you'll be busier than ever." The governor had named the former mayor of Newport to replace Jonathan, and she needed an assistant. Nancy had a stellar reputation, and Fiona Pershing, the governor's pick, had already reached out to Nancy. I was happy for her. With one final embrace, I pulled back and handed my paper ticket to the bus driver before boarding. I chose a seat at the window and gave Nancy one last wave, and watched her as she strode to her car, her posture perfect as usual. She didn't look back.

Now, with my rolling suitcase in one hand, my carry-on bag in the other, and a purse slung over my shoulder, I made my way to the Tourist Information kiosk. The area was crowded and I didn't spot her right away. But then, there she was, a woman holding a white placard that had 'J. LOGAN' printed in bold black letters. I fixed my eyes on the woman and walked toward her.

CHAPTER TWO

"I'm Jennifer Logan," I said, stopping in front of her. The woman grinned at me and tucked the placard under her left arm before extending her right hand to me.

"Good morning! I'm Bernadette Studer. Welcome to Switzerland." The woman sounded like an American. "Are you hungry? Do you need coffee?" She took the placard from under her arm and slipped it into an oversized vinyl tote bag that lay at her feet. She glanced at her wristwatch. "Our train leaves in about fifteen minutes, or we could take another one in half an hour."

"Are you American?"

"Originally, yes," she said. "Here, let me take one of your bags. I grew up in Rhode Island, but I've lived in Switzerland for years now. Sarah — she's my boss — suggested I meet with you and escort you down to Lugano. Your friend Nancy mentioned your situation to Sarah." She paused and fixed kind eyes upon me. "I'm so sorry for your loss."

As a frightened animal is tricked into a cage, I knew I couldn't run. I needed this woman, this Rhode Islander, to get me where I was headed. I couldn't do it without

11

her, and that bothered me. I steeled myself to be polite.

"Thank you," I murmured. "Could we just go to the train, please?" The sooner I arrived at the villa, the better I would feel.

"Of course," Bernadette said, shifting her weight. "But please, just sit here for one minute. I need to tell you something." She gestured to a bench and sat, turning eyes full of pleading to me.

I held tight to the handle of my rolling suitcase and stood my place. "What's wrong?" I asked, refusing to sit. Bernadette paused, then stood up. She ran a hand through the mass of copper curls on her head.

"Mrs. Logan, I'm so sorry, but the villa isn't ready for you. You see, it's usually empty in the winter months, and for some reason, the water was shut off. Unfortunately, we had a cold snap, and a pipe burst. The resulting damage must be repaired before you can move in. We have a team of men working on it right now." She stopped and took a breath. Her bottom teeth grabbed her upper lip, leaving a trace amount of coppery lipstick on them.

I said nothing for a minute, trying to absorb what she had just gushed out. I'd flown across the Atlantic Ocean and now she was telling me I couldn't move into the villa? To the place I'd paid for, in advance, for six months? In my eight years as the senator's wife, I had learned to control my emotions, so I breathed in through my nostrils and kept my face impassive as I waited for her to continue. Around us, people hurried by, everyone headed to a place that was important to them.

"Really, it shouldn't take long, and of course you'll be credited back for whatever time you're not able to live in the villa. In the meantime," she said, morphing her face into an unnaturally bright smile, "my son and his wife run a hotel in Lugano, not far from your villa. It's usually closed in January and February, but they live there year-round with their children, and they have a room for you. You'll be in Lugano, and as soon as the villa is ready, we'll arrange for you to move right in." She searched my eyes for something – acquiescence, perhaps?

How had I dealt with situations like these? There are obstacles in life, always. Would this obstacle block my way or would I step around it?

"Well, there's nothing I can do, is there? I'm here now, and at your mercy. Could we go to the train?" I was polite, I'm always polite. I didn't scream or yell or even give her dirty looks. I didn't need to. She knew.

"Yes, yes, let's go. It's this way, Mrs. Logan." She took the placard with my name on it from her tote and dropped it into a trash can.

And even though this woman Bernadette had at least twenty years on me, I never suggested she call me Jennifer. I would be Mrs. Logan. And she would be Mrs. Studer.

**

She guided me to the waiting train and we found seats. Bernadette took my suitcase and hoisted it to the rack above and, once we were situated, she pulled a bottle of water from her tote bag and offered it to me.

I shook my head and closed my eyes. I had no interest in conversation and hoped to sleep on the ride to Lugano, which Bernadette reminded me would take a couple of hours. It's not that I was rude. I wasn't a rude person. I'd been a dutiful wife to my husband, a kind and dutiful woman. I'd tried to get along with his daughter and failed. I forgave my mother for my childhood and saw that she was cared for. I deserved peace and quiet, and now I was going to live in a hotel with a family. How many children, I wondered. I didn't ask.

In spite of being exhausted, and depressed, I couldn't help but gaze out the window at the passing scenery. Once we had left behind the gray industrial buildings and factories of Zurich, the landscape transformed into fields of white. A large farmhouse sat atop a hill, with a thin trail of smoke that rose from its chimney and disappeared into a gray sky. A solitary man dressed in black led a brown horse around a fenced pen. I cut my eyes to Bernadette, who seemed engrossed in a magazine. Well, she had a view such as this every day. I was grateful for her silence.

The train stopped at a town called Zug, then skirted a lake to Arth-Goldau, then Flüelen and Göschenen. Such unfamiliar, harsh-sounding names. Each time the train stopped, I closed my eyes again. And each time I closed my eyes, I saw my husband's face. One time it was kind and smiling. Another time it was hard and cruel. Now he was at rest, and I was hoping to find peace.

When I glanced at Bernadette, she looked up and met my eyes. This time she wasn't smiling, but she did look concerned. I felt bad about shutting her out; it wasn't my nature to be mean and petty. So I spoke.

"Thank you for doing all of this for me. I know it isn't your fault that the villa can't be lived in right now. I don't blame you. It's just …" I trailed off, unable to continue. My body began to tremble and I struggled to contain myself.

She leaned forward, her elbows on her knees, and spoke to me in a low voice. "Mrs. Logan, my first husband died. It was sudden and completely unexpected.

We'd only been married a short time, so I do understand some of your grief."

She had no idea, I thought. "My husband was seventy-one years old. His illness consumed him, like a fire in the wind." Bernadette sat back against her seat. She stared out the window.

The train entered a tunnel and she told me it would be about thirty minutes before we exited.

"We're under the mountains," she said. "This tunnel is about thirty-five miles long, and just opened last month. Pretty exciting, isn't it?" Her hopeful expression dimmed when I didn't return her enthusiasm. A half hour in a tunnel? My chest tightened.

Weak fluorescent lights were our only brightness, and the noise of the train screaming through the mountain underpass drowned out any conversation. Not that I minded. I excused myself and swayed down the aisle to the bathroom at the end of the car. It was a pleasant surprise to find a toilet so spacious and clean, and I wondered if the second-class passengers enjoyed the same luxury.

The train exited its long, dark passage and we were rewarded with a brilliant blue sky. There was no more than a dusting of snow on the ground; we'd left winter behind and arrived in spring. And the names of the stations — Quinto, Faido, Bellinzona. It was as if we had traveled to Italy.

"This region is known as Ticino," Bernadette said. "Italian is the official language here."

"I don't speak Italian," I said. "Do you?"

She smiled, and there were small lines at the outer corners of her eyes. I imagined she smiled a lot, and didn't worry about the lines. Something to strive for, I thought. Laugh lines. A face well-lived. I had plenty of time still.

"*Pochissimo.* Very little," she said. "You'll be surprised, Jennifer. You'll pick it up quickly. Do you speak Spanish? Or French?"

It was the first time she'd used my first name, but unlike the attitude I had earlier, I didn't mind. It was silly to have her call me Mrs. Logan, as if I was still someone important. Here I wanted to be no one. Just Jennifer.

"I'm afraid not. My high-school French is mostly forgotten. I'm better at reading the words than speaking them. And the only Italian I can understand is likely to be on a menu."

She smiled. "I'm sure you'll be fine. My son and daughter-in-law are fluent in English, and when you get to the villa, Francesca and Louie speak English also."

I shifted in my seat. There wasn't much I could do about the hotel situation with her son, and I vowed to be a gracious and appreciative guest. I just hoped the villa repairs would take less than two weeks' time. But once I settled in at the villa, I wanted solitude.

"You know, I'm very self-sufficient. I'm sure I don't need these other people, what did you say? Francesca and Louie?"

Bernadette pulled a curl at her temple. "Well, they come with the rental."

"But I don't need ..."

She leaned forward again and pressed her palms together. I tensed. "Jennifer, they come with the rental. This is work for them. Normally they don't have much work in the winter months, so it's a good thing. Francesca is an excellent cook and housekeeper. Louie does all the maintenance around the property, and he can drive you into town. They're very much looking forward to meeting you. But you will have all the alone time you need."

I gave her a small nod of acquiescence. The train slowed as it neared our destination. Outside, it looked more like May than late January. Arching palm trees fluttered under a brilliant sun. A woman in a cotton dress hung sheets on a clothesline, and another emptied a bucket of water into a small garden. The train screeched to a stop and Bernadette rose from her seat, careful not to hit her head on the overhead luggage rack. She pulled down my rolling suitcase and set it on the floor as a recorded voice announced our arrival in Lugano, first in Italian and followed by English. No French or German, I noted.

"You packed light," Bernadette said. "You must be accustomed to traveling." I smiled but didn't affirm or deny her observation.

This is it, I thought, and trailed her out of the first-class cabin. I stepped down to the platform and seared the image into my memory. There were a few people on the platform, not many. All the signs were in Italian: *binario, biglietti, bagagli.* I had a lot to learn.

Bernadette turned to me. "I can call a taxi if you want, but it's mild today and the hotel isn't too far, if you'd like a walk. Your choice."

We took a few steps into the sun. It warmed my face. I closed my eyes and lifted my chin to the sky. After sitting on the plane and then the train for hours, it felt good to be standing. Movement would be satisfying.

"Let's walk," I said, and with a slight nod, Bernadette led the way inside the station. She stopped at a ticket booth and purchased two tickets.

"I thought we were walking," I said.

"We will. But first we'll take the funicular to the downtown area. Ah, here it is."

A tram car arrived on a slanted track. It looked capable of seating no more than a few dozen passengers, and I followed Bernadette into the car. This, she explained, was how most people in town traveled from the train station, at the top of a hill, to the downtown area closer to the lake. After a few minutes' wait, we took off.

"This was originally powered by water," Bernadette said as we began a slow descent. "It's simple physics — the weight of this car helps to propel the car at the bottom up the hill. We'll meet at the midway point."

There was a conductor, but he didn't seem to do anything. "He doesn't steer?" I whispered. "It just runs on its own power?"

She shook her head, and curls bounced around like copper springs. "There's a cable, and a pulley, and electricity now. I believe this line began operations in the late 1800s. There are quite a few funiculars in Switzerland, Jennifer."

Sure enough, another car met us at the exact midpoint, and continued to climb as our car descended to the bottom. The entire trip only took a few minutes.

When the car stopped, we exited on the side that opened. I let Bernadette take my carry-on bag and tried rolling my rectangular suitcase over bumpy cobblestones, but gave up and carried it until we reached smooth pavement. The streets were lined with small shops and cafés. Each window display seemed to outdo the previous one. Even a shop window for power tools looked extravagant and meticulously-decorated. Bernadette turned once to ask, "Do you need to stop?" I shook my head no, anxious to get to the hotel, where I intended to hole up.

We turned a corner and I saw the lake for the first time, blue and sparkly under the afternoon sun. I had rented a villa on the lake, I knew that much, but what about the hotel? Would I be near the lake? I hoped so.

We arrived in a public square ringed by trees. Leafless in winter, they were unusually stubby.

"I don't think I've ever seen trees like that," I remarked.

"They're quite common here," Bernadette replied. "I learned about it myself. The upper branches are pruned, which makes them look like that. It's more common in the towns and cities, mostly to keep a uniform height. Once they're in foliage, they look normal!"

I'd worked up a sweat under the sun. There were no

clouds in the sky and only the slightest of breezes off the lake. Small cars were parked in a neat row along one edge of the square, and I noted the absence of typically oversized American vehicles. A couple of men sat at a table outside a café, smoking cigarettes and drinking beer from narrow glasses. A caramel-colored dog lay at the feet of one of the men. We skirted by, walked another half block, and arrived at the front door of the hotel.

CHAPTER THREE

A sign on the glass door read '*Chiuso* — Closed' and Bernadette pulled out her phone. After a few seconds, she laughed and said, "We're right outside!" She disconnected and said, "Lucia will be right down to let us in. She's very excited to meet you!"

Lucia. That must be her daughter-in-law, her son's wife. Her son must have married a Swiss woman to be living here, I imagined. But I didn't care enough to ask. I hoped she didn't think me rude not to show any interest in her family. I was sure I'd learn more than I needed or wanted to know in the two weeks I'd be living with them all.

A pretty woman about my age unlocked the door from the inside, and the weight of our bodies on the outside doormat opened the automatic door with a whoosh.

"Mama," she crooned to Bernadette as they kissed each other on the cheek, first the left, then the right, and then the left again. Pulling away, the younger woman turned to face me and held out her hand. In a soft voice with a light Italian accent, she said, "Welcome to the hotel, Mrs. Logan. I'm sorry your villa is not ready for you at this time, but you are most welcome here at the Hotel Walter." She said 'Walter' like 'Valter.' "I am Lucia, Michel's wife, and – oh! Here is my Isabella. Bella, your nonna is here! Give her a big kiss. And say hello to Mrs. Logan."

A little girl I guessed to be five or six stepped out from behind her mother and gave Bernadette a face-splitting grin. "Nonny!" she cried in her little-girl, high-pitched voice. The voice of an angel, I thought. With light blue eyes and a head of blonde ringlets, she was adorable. "You are not my nonny." The little girl shook her head and narrowed her round blue eyes at me.

"No, she is not your nonny, Bella, but she is staying with us for a little while." Lucia spoke English to the girl, who probably could speak Italian as well, I imagined. Lucia turned to me and said, "I have your room ready, Mrs. Logan. Here, let me help you with that bag." She reached to take my suitcase, but I wouldn't let her. Keeping control of a six-year-old was hard enough.

"I'm fine, really. Your daughter is beautiful."

"Thank you. My sons are still in school, but they'll be home in time for dinner. Please, come with me."

Bernadette and I followed Lucia past the deserted reception desk to a tiny elevator, where we all squeezed in. Lucia held Isabella in her arms and I balanced my suitcase on my feet so the door would close. I glanced at a metal sign affixed inside the elevator that said something about 200kg and assumed that was the maximum weight allowed inside the little box. Doing quick calculations in my head, I estimated we were within the acceptable limits. The elevator inched its way up.

"I put you on the top floor," Lucia said in an apologetic voice. "We live on the ground floor, behind the restaurant, but I know we can be loud at times, and I understand you want peace and quiet." With a quick glance to Bernadette, Lucia lowered her already-soft voice to just above a whisper. "I'm very sorry about your husband."

I took a deep breath through my nose. Another person who knows my story. I wondered how much Bernadette had told her. How much did Bernadette know? Had they done online research about Jonathan, about me? "Thank you," I said and looked at the floor. Please, please no more questions.

We reached the fourth floor and the elevator came to a shuddering stop. Bernadette pulled the iron gate aside and pushed open the door. I staggered into the hallway, relieved to be out of that claustrophobic space. Isabella led the way down the long hallway, skipping ahead of her mother and Bernadette, who walked a step in front of me. At the end of the corridor, in eerie quiet, Lucia unlocked and opened the door to my room. It was probably spacious by Swiss hotel standards, especially a hotel as old as the Walter. The end room held a double bed, one plump, upholstered chair, and a good-sized desk. French doors opened onto a balcony and I did indeed have a view of the lake. It was beautiful, I had to admit.

There were fresh flowers on the bedside table and a small rectangular box on the bed. Isabella hopped on one foot, then the other, until Lucia smiled and laid a gentle hand on her daughter's head.

"Bella is excited that you're here and would like you to open the box, please."

When I leaned over to pick up the box, Isabella clapped her hands and said something I didn't understand. Beneath the bright paper was a box of chocolates with the word 'Läderach' on the lid. Inside lay nine exquisite pieces of chocolate — dark, milk, and white. I glanced at Isabella and then looked to her mother. "Would your daughter like to choose one?" I asked with a wink.

"Oh no, Mrs. Logan, those are for you. Bella has plenty of chocolate downstairs. But she did help to pick them out for you."

I left the box covered and crouched down to look Isabella in the eye. "*Grazie*, Isabella," I said, in the only Italian I knew, and hoped the little girl understood my accent. She threw her arms around me and again gurgled in high-pitched Italian that made no sense to me. I couldn't remember the last time a child had embraced me.

"The room is very nice. Thank you again," I said to Lucia, then looked to Bernadette to include her in my acknowledgement. It wasn't my villa, but it wasn't bad, either.

"We'll let you get settled," Lucia said to me. "You'll have dinner with us tonight? Please?"

My first night in Lugano, when I knew nothing of the city? "Yes, of course. Thank you."

"Wonderful! Dinner is at six, in the restaurant." Lucia turned to her mother-in-law. "Mama? Can you stay?"

"No, I'm afraid not. Gerard expects me back home this evening. I'll catch the next train out." She extended her hand to me, and when I took it, she impulsively pulled me into an embrace. I'd had two hugs in the space of five minutes.

"Jennifer," she said close to my ear, "I will keep in touch, and I'll be in contact with the guys at the villa every day. You may even get in there earlier than the two weeks, but I do hope your stay here will be a comfort." She pulled back and searched my eyes. "I'm sorry about everything you've had to go through since you arrived this morning. Truly. Here, let me give you my cell number." She started to reach in her purse but I stopped her.

"I don't have a cell phone," I said, noting the startled expressions on the faces of both women. It made me smile. "I don't want one. At all. No one needs to reach me, believe me. And I don't want to be reached, anyway." I guess I didn't need to add that last line. But I made my point.

Both women nodded solemnly without looking at each other. "Well, I'll be back when it's time to move you into the villa, if not sooner." And before I could protest, Bernadette had left, leaving me standing in my hotel room with Lucia and her little daughter.

"*Va bene*," Lucia said. "We will see you at six, Mrs. Logan."

As she turned to walk out the door, I called after her. "Please, call me Jennifer."

"*Ciao*, Jennifer!" Little Isabella waved at me and ran

out the door into the hallway.

**

What I really wanted to do was sleep. It was three in the afternoon and dinner was three hours away. A little nap would do me good, but I'd been warned. Bernadette had implored me, back on the train, to try not to sleep until it was a normal bedtime in Lugano. "I know it'll be hard, especially since you didn't get much sleep on the airplane," she'd said, "but you'll throw off your body rhythms. I did that once, lying down in the mid-afternoon, and I slept until two in the morning. Then I was wide awake."

Instead, I showered, changed into clean clothes, and put on my walking shoes. I would stroll by the lake, and take advantage of the mild weather. According to Bernadette, the temperatures were unusual for January.

"Does it ever snow in Lugano?" I'd asked her.

"Sure, it snows here," she'd assured me. "This warm spell is not normal. But our climate is changing, isn't it? January typically is cool, not icy cold. Still, you won't see tourists around here until maybe late March or early April."

"Good," I'd muttered.

I picked up the key to my room and locked the door

behind me. Most hotels now used credit card-type room keys, but Walter was a throwback to old times, so a key seemed appropriate. I walked past the empty reception desk and tried to leave the hotel. But the glass door was locked. Of course, because the hotel was closed. I sighed. Was I to be a prisoner? I took a few steps back to the reception desk and looked for a buzzer, a bell, something to get Lucia's attention. Finding nothing, I climbed a short flight of stairs next to the elevator and followed the sign that pointed to the restaurant. There, I found Lucia setting a table for six, placing wine glasses and silverware. I cleared my throat and she jumped.

"I'm sorry," I said. "I didn't mean to startle you."

"Oh, Jennifer! I thought you'd be sleeping."

"Bernadette said it was a bad idea to sleep. She said it would throw off my body clock or something."

Lucia laughed. "Yes, she's right. It would." She set down the last of the spoons. "How can I help you?"

I tugged at my jacket. "I thought I'd take a walk by the lake on such a pretty day. But I can't get out of the hotel."

"Oh no! You're right. Come with me, I'll show you the way."

I followed Lucia back downstairs and she ducked

30

behind the reception desk. She took another key from a drawer and handed it to me. "This key will unlock the side door," she said, pointing straight ahead. "You'll see it when you're outside. When the hotel is open, our employees use it for entry. The key will let you in and the door will lock behind you."

I took the key, thanked her, and she showed me the way to the side door. Once outside, I gulped fresh air and tried to ease the heaviness I felt in my chest. And why? Lucia was lovely, she couldn't have been more gracious. I used a bright yellow crosswalk to traverse the street to the lakeside. A small kiosk, shuttered for the winter, stood sentry along the lonely lake. Pedal boats lay dormant, covered in blue tarpaulins, and two pigeons had the dock all to themselves. There were people out walking, of course, taking advantage of the mild weather. An old woman in a headscarf walked an ugly bulldog. Two boys either playing hooky from school or just finished with classes for the day loped along the walkway, chortling over something only young boys would find funny. A thirtyish businessman with a brown ponytail and fine, Italian-looking shoes hurried past. I strolled the promenade and stopped often to stare at the mirrorlike expanse of water, or the mountains that rose up from the shores. I wasn't sure where my villa was, but I wanted to see it. I approached a woman sitting alone on one of the benches. Her head was bent and I wasn't sure if she was awake.

"Excuse me," I said. I stood in front of her and blocked the sun. She lifted her head and removed her sunglasses. One eye was discolored slightly, in light purple and yellow, as if a bruise was healing. I tried not to focus on it. "Do you know the Villa del Sol?"

She stared at me for a moment, then shook her head, replaced her sunglasses, and lowered her head toward her chest. Perhaps I had awakened her. I walked away.

There was a café not far from the promenade, next to a Burger King, of all places. I took a seat outside in the sun and waited for a white-aproned waiter to approach.

"*Prego,*" he said.

"Coffee?" With a sharp nod, he disappeared back inside the café and reappeared a moment later, carrying a tray. He set the tray on my table. On it was a white saucer, a white cup two-thirds full of thick, black liquid, and a small spoon. He added a little silver creamer and a small glass box full of sugar 'straws.' The tray was uncomplicated, but the process was elaborate, all for a simple cup of coffee. I thought about the people at home who carried their cardboard cups of coffee like scepters. Walk and sip.

"*Prego,*" he said again and moved to another table.

I prepared my coffee, adding plenty of cream. After a sip, I emptied two of the sugar straws into the little cup. Perhaps I should have asked for decaf. I could feel the caffeine course through my veins. My senses sharpened.

The next time the waiter passed by my table, I raised my hand and waited for him to stop. "Do you know the Villa del Sol?" I asked, not even trying to speak Italian. I'd learn it, eventually.

"Villa del Sol?" He stared out across the lake and stroked a nonexistent beard. "Del Sol," he said again before shaking his head. "No, *signora. Non lo so.*"

Without an address, I wouldn't be able to find it. I sipped my coffee and watched people pass by. The women were so fashionable — skinny jeans and an oversized turtleneck sweater, a faux shearling jacket paired with a pencil skirt and boots. My clothes were those of a senator's wife — neutral and classic. Boring. I'd learned the hard, humiliating way that being Jonathan's wife meant never wearing anything too tight, too revealing to public events, not even to dinner with his friends. At twenty-six, I'd had to change from a mini-dress and boots to a long-sleeved gray silk sheath and sensible heels. Having my husband tell me I was dressed like a streetwalker was a rebuke I never forgot. The way I dressed had caught his eye in the first place, but once we were married, it was as if he wanted me to be someone else.

My mind was filled with memories that I couldn't erase. I came to this place by the lake in an effort to quell the constant churning of remembrance, of love lost, then found, then tested.

The light of the afternoon was growing flat. The days were still short in late January, and I headed back to the hotel. I had a second wind, likely from the espresso, and didn't feel at all sleepy, for which I was grateful, as I expected I'd have to participate in dinner conversation. I had yet to meet Lucia's husband, this boy of Bernadette's, and the two sons. A happy family. I quickened my pace.

CHAPTER FOUR

Lucia brought a steaming casserole dish to the table. She lifted the glass cover to reveal pasta with meat and tomato sauce. Her eldest, who was called Jean-Bernard, carried a large wooden bowl filled with salad greens. He was followed by his younger brother, Luca. Luca placed a bottle of olive oil and a bottle of balsamic vinegar on the table. Finally, Jean-Michel, who preferred to be called just Michel, set two bottles of red wine next to his place.

I watched the procession, as I was told in no uncertain terms that I was to sit and relax. Lucia had introduced me to the men in her family as I entered the dining room, which was a long room with tall windows on the wall that faced the street and lake. There were about twelve tables, but only one was in use — our table, closest to the kitchen and separated from the rest of the area, set with a blue and white tablecloth.

Once everyone was seated, Lucia nodded to her husband, who turned to me. "I hope it does not offend you, Jennifer, but we offer a prayer before our meal."

I was startled, not so much by the admission but by

the fact that he seemed to care if I might be offended. "Of course I'm not offended," I said, looking around at the children. "I'm pleased." It was true. My history didn't include an intact family praying and eating together, but I was raised Catholic by my dear grandpa, and I found the ritual comforting. I clasped my hands in my lap and bowed my head.

"Jean-Bernard," Michel said, "it's your turn tonight."

The boy, who at thirteen had the russet hair of his father and the soft features of his mother, cast his eyes downward and spoke. *"Benedici, Signore, noi e questi tuoi doni, che stiamo per ricevere dalla tua generosità. Per Cristo nostro Signore."*

I made the sign of the cross with everyone else, and the quiet of the prayer morphed into excited chatter. Michel used an enormous spoon to heap a mound of the pasta on each plate as it was passed to him, mine first. Lucia offered the bowl of salad to me, and I used silver tongs to place lettuce leaves on my plate, then drizzled deep green olive oil and dark balsamic vinegar over them. Michel passed a basket of aromatic garlic bread to me, and even though I hadn't eaten bread for the past two years, I took a slice and smiled. I wouldn't worry so much about bread, or pasta, anymore, I told myself. Being in the public eye had made me afraid to gain even a few pounds, but that was no longer the case. There were no reporters around to publicly wonder if I was pregnant ('Will the senator be a father again at seventy?'). I bit into the warm, buttery bread and savored its texture. If garlic bread could soothe my troubled soul, I was definitely in the right place.

"This is delicious," I said after the first mouthful. I'd forgotten how wonderful it was to eat home-cooked food. When was the last time I'd made dinner in our house? I had no idea. In the beginning of our marriage, Jonathan flew home every weekend, and I took great pains to prepare lavish meals for him. I pretended I was Ina Garten, cooking for her beloved Jeffrey. Usually, we went out on Saturday night — there was always an invitation waiting, and on Friday nights Jonathan was too tired to enjoy much, so I'd make dinner for early Sunday afternoon. Roast pork, turkey with all the trimmings, grilled swordfish in the summer. I taught myself how to cook by watching videos online. During our first two or three years of marriage, Jonathan would eat. He'd even compliment me on my cooking skills.

"Thank you! I'm glad you like it, Jennifer. I wasn't sure what to make for your first meal in Switzerland." Lucia beamed at me, so obviously happy that she'd succeeded, and I understood how important it was to pay the cook a compliment.

"Have you stayed awake since you arrived this morning?" Michel asked as he filled my glass with dark ruby-red wine.

I smiled. "I've been up since five o'clock yesterday morning. I really didn't sleep on the plane, and I was warned — repeatedly — about sleeping this afternoon." I winked at Lucia, whose look of alarm was quickly replaced with a grin.

"Well, you should have no trouble sleeping tonight, I'm sure. You're far away from this rowdy bunch. And I know it's been said many times already, but we are very sorry about your villa."

"Oh, it's not your fault."

"No, of course not, but I understand you had a different expectation about your first days here in Lugano, and living in a hotel with a family of five was not part of that plan."

They were all trying so hard, I thought. I needed to be sure they understood how grateful I was. No more cool aloof Jennifer, devoid of passion or emotion. I'm not raising three children. I'm not constantly interrupted during mealtime by a six-year-old, and a ten-year-old. I've never had to balance a career with motherhood. Lucia may not work outside the hotel, but when the hotel is open, she's busy all the time, overseeing the housekeeping staff, troubleshooting what dilemmas must arise during the day. All I wanted was to be alone. And I would get to the villa eventually. Meanwhile, I couldn't deny that I was enjoying dinner with the Eicher family.

No one allowed me to help clean up; in fact, Michel and his two boys cleared the dishes as he insisted Lucia stay seated. Would Jonathan ever have done that? Jonathan was of a different generation, one in which he expected the woman to maintain the household. I was sure that his first wife had done just that, and he had no reason to think it would be different with me. Michel was my age, and it looked perfectly normal that he and his sons cleared the plates and brought the dishes into the kitchen.

"You have a lovely family," I said to Lucia, meaning it. "Have you always lived here in Lugano?"

"Oh, no!" she replied, pulling a sleepy Isabella onto her lap. "But I first met Michel here. He was working as an apprentice right in this hotel, and I was vacationing with my parents. We lived in Milan but came here frequently in the summer. Then Michel and I married and moved to Fribourg. Do you know Fribourg? It's about midway between Geneva and Zurich, and that's where Bernadette found Michel."

I shook my head slightly, not comprehending. "Found him? Isn't he her son?"

Lucia stroked her daughter's hair and smiled. "Oh yes, but perhaps Bernadette did not tell you her story." I realized I hadn't asked Bernadette anything about herself on the two-hour train ride from Zurich earlier in the day. I hadn't cared. Lucia continued. "Bernadette is Michel's mother, but he was raised by his adoptive parents. I should let her tell you the story." She rocked her daughter gently and continued. "Bernadette returned to Fribourg many years later and they found each other. And now she is remarried and lives in Bern. Michel is very lucky."

"And Michel's father? His birth father?"

She drew Isabella closer and looked past me for a moment. "Ah, yes. He is no longer with us. He and Michel made, what do you say, amends."

I was curious, and something told me that Lucia would gladly fill me in, but I didn't ask any more questions. I knew what it felt like to have my privacy disregarded. If Bernadette wished to tell me her story, I would listen. Otherwise, it was time to change the subject.

"Your *cucina* is again clean, Lulu," Michel said, bending to kiss his wife's head. "Boys! Come say goodnight to Signora Logan before you leave to do your homework. Here, give her to me. I'll put her to bed." He took his nearly-asleep daughter from Lucia and lifted her high in his arms. The two boys hurried in from the kitchen and each offered me his hand in turn, saying in perfect English that it was a pleasure to meet me and they would see me the next day.

"Thank you both, so much, for a very nice dinner. I could not have been welcomed to Lugano any better than this."

"Jennifer, the kitchen is always open, if you get hungry or cannot sleep. Please take whatever you want. We will see you in the morning. *Buona notte.*"

I left them and climbed the stairs to the fourth floor, then took sleepy steps down the corridor to my room. I undressed quickly and took two minutes to brush my teeth and wash my face. Everything else could wait until morning, I thought as I dropped into a soft bed and fell asleep way ahead of my memories.

**

The days passed slowly. At times, I felt as though I was captive in the Hotel Walter, surrounded by well-meaning, cheerful people and loads of carbohydrates. On cold and rainy days, I often stayed inside my room and read, only venturing down for dinner at six. It was so quiet that even with the windows shut I could hear the church bells of San Lorenzo. After the first three days, I was left alone, having assured Lucia that no, I was fine, but I needed some quiet time to grieve.

It was a lie. I didn't need time to grieve — my husband's absence was just part of every day. In truth, I was relieved Jonathan was gone. He'd suffered terribly in the short span of his illness. There were times he'd been vile to me, his words like sabers, slicing me open, leaving me to bleed out. He had refused to let me nurse him, even as he grudgingly admitted he needed assistance. He'd allowed his aide Stephen to hire a comely woman with near-black skin and a lilting voice to provide him with personal care. Cedella arrived at our house with long skinny braids twisted and piled atop her head, and when she left, those braids were loose and swinging against her back. When she washed Jonathan, no one was allowed in the room. He listened intently to every word she spoke, and had her come to him each morning at ten. She'd been attending to my husband for less than two weeks, but there was an intimacy between them that bruised my heart. When she showed up to the house on Christmas morning, I realized that I had never even thought to call her. He was already gone — off to Thornton Read Funeral Home on the other side of town.

**

On the days that it didn't rain, I left the hotel right after breakfast. My hosts rose early, I knew, so I usually waited until nine o'clock to head downstairs for coffee. I tidied my room, rinsed out the bathtub, folded my towels. I told Lucia the bedding was clean, the towels still fresh.

There was always fresh fruit, jams, butter, sliced bread and croissants. I suspected that Lucia was stationed somewhere behind the dining room, aware of my entrance but keeping her distance from me, and as soon as I'd leave the dining room, I pictured her hurrying in to clear everything away. It wasn't that I wanted to alienate any of them. I made an effort to eat dinner with the family every evening while I was there.

On day eleven, a clear day with a brisk breeze blowing in off the lake, I walked back through the town to the funicular and rode up to the train station. It was the first time I'd been back, away from the lake and the Hotel Walter, and I reveled in the smells — diesel fumes from delivery trucks, a woman's heavy perfume (there she was, down the platform), buttery bread from the bakery next door. I perused the yellow board showing *partenze*. A train to Lucerne, nonstop, left in twenty minutes. Without stopping to plan, I bought a ticket and found my track, where the train stood waiting.

Perhaps it was because I'd been stuck at the hotel.

Maybe it was wanderlust borne of my frustration at not being able to get into the villa. I didn't focus on the why. I just knew I needed to be going somewhere.

Heading north and away from the rain, we entered the long tunnel and I was plunged into blackness. The train made a high-pitched whine as it sped under the mountain, but when we emerged on the other side, there was snow on the ground, just as it had been the day I landed and traveled from Zurich with Bernadette. We passed farmland and fields covered in white. The landscape was devoid of color, yet I found it comforting, like being wrapped in a soft gray blanket. It was as if there were two Switzerlands — one north of the tunnel, full of clouds and snow, and the other one, mild and sunny to the south.

At Lucerne, I exited the train. There was a lake across from the station, but low-lying clouds obscured any views. I bought a cheese sandwich and a bottle of fizzy water at a takeaway stand and looked at the board for another place to go. No more *partenze*, now the yellow board listed *Abfahrt/Départ*. Bern was the capital of Switzerland. I purchased another ticket and found my train. Once aboard, I took an empty seat in a nearly-empty compartment. A passenger across from me unwrapped a sandwich, so I followed her lead and ate my lunch on board, while I waited for the train to depart. The train pulled away on time and we inched out of the station. Between bites, I stared out the window at concrete walls full of graffiti, cartoonish more than obscene. There was an insurance company, a high-rise apartment building, then another apartment building. Within minutes, the train had picked up speed. It skirted an ice-covered lake. Snowy hills rose above the lake, and higher still, mountains with winding ski trails carved into them, only half-visible under low-lying clouds.

But where was the sun? Not here, certainly. I thought about the Villa del Sol and its promise of sun. I still hadn't heard from Bernadette, eleven days in.

The train stopped at Sursee, at the edge of the lake. Some passengers exited the train as others stepped on. Once more, we pulled away, past more farmland and snow and nondescript beige and gray apartment buildings. I searched for color and found none. This could be a difficult place to live in the winter, I thought.

There was more English on the signage, more than I expected. A bar called 'Part of the Family.' A boutique called 'Sea Horse.' 'Rainbow Takeaway.' But on the train, all I heard spoken was Swiss German, a singsongy dialect that sounded nothing like the German with which I was vaguely familiar. I couldn't understand it, so I rode in silence. Conversations drifted past me like the tiny snowflakes outside my window.

The train pulled into Wauwil and dropped off a few more passengers on the platform, then started up again and gathered speed as it headed toward its next stop. We paralleled a road and I counted only one car and one truck. Most people used public transportation, and I understood why. I didn't miss driving, even though the traffic back home was much worse.

Each village was marked with a spired church. Little hamlets clustered around the church, and chalets dotted the hillsides above. We passed industrial areas. A Wüest crane made a giant T in the sky. Factories with names I didn't know — Galliker, Misapor, Emmi. Oh, Emmi — the yogurt. I recognized that one.

We flew through Brittnau, a tiny station that didn't even deserve a stop, and halted in Zofingen. There were but a few passengers to embark, and only one from my car who left. Within the minute, the train shut its doors and was back on its way. I spotted a castle's turret from the train window and made a mental note to research the town. Perhaps it would be worth a visit one day. But I remembered my villa. I hadn't even seen it yet. Still, I thought, perhaps one day I would return to Zofingen and look at the castle.

As the train picked up speed once again, the same ticket collector walked through each car and announced the next stop. He remembered me, and the passengers who had already shown him their ticket. He must have a very good memory. Or else he assumed that the new passengers would simply show their tickets. What if someone boarded the train without a ticket? Surely he would know. There is a lot of trust, I realized.

I dug around in my bag and found Bernadette's business card. I thought that perhaps I would arrive, unannounced, and demand entry into my villa. Even the fantasy of it made me smile. So unlike me. Jennifer Logan. Mrs. Jonathan Logan. Jennifer, wife of Senator Logan. No, I'm not his daughter, I'm his wife. As if we were the only May-December couple in the world.

Finally, the train arrived in Bern. It was already mid-afternoon and I knew I should plan my return journey. Lucia and Michel would be worried if I didn't show up for dinner at six. I asked at the ticket counter and was told it was a three-hour ride, with changes, back to Lugano. The earliest I could leave was three o'clock. I checked my watch. The train left in ten minutes. I had just spent the entire day riding trains.

"Fine," I said. "One ticket to Lugano, please. On the next train." She processed my request and I turned on my heel to walk back to the platforms.

If I were in the villa, it wouldn't matter. I could come and go as I pleased, and not be beholden to anyone's feelings. I knew I'd be late for dinner, and I had no way to contact either of them. How smart had I been to think I could live without my phone?

There was a bar in the middle of the train, a dining car. I found a seat there and ordered wine.

CHAPTER FIVE

By the time the train arrived in Lugano, I'd consumed more wine than I should have, and hailed a taxi to take me to the hotel. I didn't trust myself in the dark.

"*L'albergo è chiuso, signora,*" the taxi driver said, eyeing me in his rearview mirror. "The hotel is closed," he added, after I didn't respond.

"Yes, I know. Please take me there anyway."

I let myself in through the side door and stumbled up the stairs into the dining room. They were at the table, eating. I was relieved; I'd have felt bad if they were waiting for me.

Michel stood as I hurried across the empty dining room. "Are you alright, Jennifer?" I took off my coat and tossed it onto an empty table. He pulled out my chair for me, so thoughtful, always.

"I'm sorry, please forgive me." I knew I was tipsy, and tried hard to enunciate, which probably made my inebriation more obvious.

Lucia focused her attention on Isabella's food, which she cut into tiny pieces. "You needn't apologize, Jennifer," she said, the edges of her voice clipped. "You are not obligated to dine with us." She raised her eyes to me and I saw the hurt reflected there. Oh, dear. These people had been so kind to me.

"I rode the train today and time escaped me. I'm sorry if I worried you."

Lucia returned her focus on Isabella. How odd, I thought, that being late for one meal in eleven days would turn her against me. The boys seemed oblivious to the drama, but Michel was the voice of reason.

"We were just concerned, that's all," he said, holding the bottle of wine aloft until I nodded. He poured some of the golden liquid into my goblet. Wine was the last thing I needed, but I drank it anyway. "Tell us of your travels, Jennifer."

I took a sip and was about to recount my poorly planned journey to Bern when I was interrupted.

"I don't understand why you don't have a phone. Everyone has a phone. You really should get one." Lucia's eyes were shiny and I was touched, but stupefied, that one small event could bring her to tears.

"Okay, Lulu," Michel said in a near-whisper. The

boys had paused and were staring at their mother.

If I were in my villa, it wouldn't even be an issue, I thought, stabbing a carrot with my fork. I did not wish to be obligated to anyone, but there I was, still a prisoner in their lovely hotel, held captive by the nicest people one could imagine.

"Perhaps I will get one," I murmured softly, and ate as quickly as I could, before thanking Lucia profusely and, feigning exhaustion, bid the Eicher family an early good night.

**

On day thirteen, Bernadette arrived with the good news. The villa was ready and I could move in.

"Louie will be here in an hour with his truck and he'll drive you to your new home." Bernadette beamed at me. "Everything is in working order. I was there this morning to confirm. This evening you'll be sleeping in a new bed." She and I stood in the dining room as Lucia moved around us, clearing the table in silence.

Lucia and I had been tiptoeing around each other for the past two days, ever since I had arrived late for dinner. I still felt like a child who'd been scolded by her mother and was feeling her way tentatively, to see if she could get back in her mother's good graces. It was ridiculous.

I wondered if she'd disappear when it was time for me to leave.

"Will you come with me?" I asked. "Please, Bernadette, I'd like for you to accompany me."

"Oh, you don't have to worry about Louie! He's very kind."

I stiffened. "I'm not worried about him. But I'd like for you, as my rental agent, to come with me. Will you do that?" I tightened my jaw. I needed to get away from everybody — Bernadette with her over-bright smile, Lucia with the drama. Enough already with all of them. And I intended to keep Louie and Francesca at arm's length as well. No getting close to my employees.

Bernadette's cheeks turned pink at my rebuke. "Of course I'll come with you. I'll give you time to pack." She exited the dining room into what I assumed was the family's residence. I wouldn't know; I'd never been invited back there. Maybe Lucia was a terrible housekeeper. It didn't matter.

I climbed the stairs and returned to my room on the fourth floor and packed my clothes in the bags I'd brought with me. I stripped the bed and lightly folded the linens, leaving them on the bare mattress, then used the bathroom one more time and took the towels and washcloth and left them on the side of the tub. I would have done the laundry myself if I could have, anything to leave the room in pristine condition. Lucia would never be able to tell Bernadette that I was messy.

At five minutes before the set time, and no sooner, I descended the elevator to the ground floor and found Bernadette leaning on the reception desk, engaged in cheery conversation with Lucia. Next to them stood a man with a face like a weathered board.

All three of them turned to me. I focused only on Lucia and beamed until she gave me a small smile in return before lowering her eyes.

"Jennifer, this is Louie," Bernadette said, as the man nodded. He wore a black fisherman's cap that couldn't hide bushy gray eyebrows and dark eyes that reminded me of black jelly beans. He squinted at me and I offered my hand. He took it, and his was dry and rough, as I imagined it would be.

"Hello," I said, holding his gaze. His was in my employ, and I needed to establish my authority from the beginning. Kindness could come later.

"*Signora*," he said, lowering his chin as he did. "This is all?" He gestured to the suitcase I had wheeled out of the elevator. My carry-on bag was still in my left hand.

"And this," I said, lifting the bag slightly. I turned to

Bernadette. "I'll ride with you." It was not a question, and Bernadette nodded. Then I took a step closer to Lucia.

"Lucia. I'm sorry I'll miss saying goodbye to Michel and your children. Thank you for your hospitality these past two weeks. I do appreciate everything, you know." I touched her upper arm and felt the boniness of her limb through the thin fabric of her shirt.

She threw her skinny arms around me and I pressed my palms against her prominent shoulder blades. "You were the perfect guest! I will miss you, Jennifer, and I do hope you come to visit us once you're settled. You know you're always welcome here."

I swallowed hard and nodded. "*Grazie. Mille grazie*, Lucia." We had little in common, she and I. Although we were close in age, she reveled in motherhood. She was sweet, and pure, and good. I couldn't imagine that we'd ever be friends; the differences between our pasts and presents were too grand. Still, I liked her. I liked her family. And I was grateful to know people in Lugano.

Louie wheeled the suitcase to his truck and hoisted it into the open bed. I tossed my carry-on in next to it, then glanced up to the sky, but there was barely a single cloud. I suppose we could have simply put the bags in the trunk of Bernadette's car. Louie really wasn't necessary, but I suppose he needed to feel that he was.

"Bernadette," I said as we climbed into her sedan. "You drive a car. I didn't realize. Why did you pick me up at the airport and why did we take the train down here? Why didn't you drive?"

She smiled. "I prefer the train, actually. You might think it funny, because I'm American, but I've lived here for so long that I'd much rather take a train than drive a car. When I'm on the train, I can work, or read. Today, I have other stops to make, and the car will get me there faster." She shrugged and shifted the car into drive. "Come on, let's go to your villa."

CHAPTER SIX

The Villa del Sol was built in the 1920s, and like other grand homes in the area, it was decidedly Italian in design. We pulled up to wrought-iron gates at the front of the house, while Louie drove up a narrow driveway on the side that led to a large parking area in the back.

"It's nice, isn't it?" Bernadette asked in a soft voice. I could only nod in agreement. I had lived in a house that I always thought was too big for just Jonathan and me, but the villa was easily twice as large.

"This is the main entrance, and I wanted you to get the full effect today, but you may end up using the back door to come and go." She pointed up the hill to the spot where Louie had parked his truck. "The back entrance leads into the kitchen. Louie and Francesca live in the apartment behind the villa — you can't see it from here, but I'll show you." She led me up the ornate stairs to the massive front door and twisted a large brass knob. "You first, Jennifer!"

I stepped inside and caught my breath. The floor's intricate black and white marble was exquisitely laid out in a bold geometric design. The doors were ornately-carved heavy oak, and moldings, also ornate, surrounded the entrances and hallways. On the ground floor was a spacious living room at the front of the villa, with tall windows that provided unlimited views of the lake and plenty of natural light. A small dining room was next to the living room, also with tall windows, similar to what I'd seen at the Hotel Walter. High ceilings and tall windows — I imagined it might be cold and drafty, but a fireplace set into the wall looked promising. The furnishings were plush and inviting — I pictured myself curled up on the sofa with a cup of tea and a good book. Toward the back of the house near the kitchen was a toilet and sink, a 'WC' as Bernadette called it, with pink-and-white striped wallpaper and gleaming white fixtures.

"The kitchen is in the back," Bernadette said, using her arm to sweep back toward the rear of the house. "Francesca will be by later to prepare your dinner." Before I could protest, she raised her index finger. "Jennifer, it's all been discussed. This is how it will be. Neither Francesca nor Louie will be in your way." Her eyes were hard and flinty, but she softened her admonition with a smile. "Come on, I want to show you the rest of the house."

We walked back to the main hallway, where a curving staircase with a wrought-iron banister wound its way to the second floor. The stairs, like the entryway floor, were marble, with patterned runners on each step. I wondered if anyone had slipped on those steps and was grateful for the traction provided by the runners.

"Follow me." Bernadette began climbing and I followed her, up twenty or so steps to the second floor. She led me through the master bedroom to a large sunny bathroom, big enough to waltz in. A huge white claw-foot tub sat in the middle of the room. I imagined it could hold four people, and I let my mind wander. It was as if the Roaring Twenties had been a big part of this home. Bathtub gin, flappers floating in and out of rooms, couples draped over each other.

"Jennifer?" Bernadette roused me from my daydream and I felt my neck grow warm.

"It's...lovely," I stammered. Two tall windows reached from a couple of inches above the floor almost to the ceiling, and there was the lake again. I could lounge in the giant bathtub and still see the lake. We crossed back into the master bedroom, where Louie had set my big suitcase on the floor at the foot of the bed. The floor was parquet, a geometric mosaic of wood pieces that formed stars around the bed. And the bed! A four-poster behemoth that required a step to climb into, it was covered in a puffy white duvet. I would love the bed, and maybe I'd even sleep again.

"I don't know what your house in Providence was like, Jennifer, but you seem to like the villa so far, yes?"

"Yes," I murmured.

The house on Cooke Street where I lived with Jonathan was built in the 1820s by a man named Obadiah Blanding. There was a rectangular white plaque next to the front door with that information, and many of the old houses in our area bore similar plaques — a project by the Providence Preservation Society. Jonathan was so proud of his house, with its gray paint and white trim, its widow's walk and red door. I didn't really care one way or another; the history of the old house had nothing to do with me. Besides, I never thought of it as mine in any way. It was his, and before that it was his and Virginia's, and then it was his again and I lived there with him.

"Come see the other rooms," she called to me. I followed her to view two guestrooms. I would not have guests in my villa, no. Each of the guest bedrooms had its own bathroom, both with antique fixtures. "There are gardens, still dormant, of course," Bernadette said. "Louie tends to them. Are you a gardener?"

I shook my head no. I was never a gardener, preferring to arrange flowers that had already been pulled or cut from their dirt beds.

"And one more flight," Bernadette said as she led me

to a back staircase. "This will take you down to the kitchen or up to the third floor. The top floor was most likely used for servant quarters, back in the day."

We climbed the stairs, wooden, not marble, to an open floor. There was a treadmill situated near the windows in front. Not tall windows, these were normal-sized and flanked by thin white curtains. But the view! That view of the lake and surrounding areas might be enough to get me on the treadmill every morning. Maybe.

"And outside, next to the gardens, there's a pergola and swimming pool. Of course, the pool is closed for the winter, but as soon as the weather warms up enough, Louie will open it for you."

It was a huge house for just me, but I was happy. Finally, I was on my own. I could bounce off the walls, sing, dance, skip, sleep. I could come and go as I pleased. I could eat what I wanted, when I wanted. I could soak in the tub for an hour if I wished. I was beholden to no one. I exhaled and let my shoulders relax.

"It's just as I had hoped. Thank you." I held out my hand, but again Bernadette pulled me into a hug. She smelled like vanilla and cinnamon, like a kitchen at Christmastime. I closed my eyes and breathed.

"I hope it provides the quiet peace you're looking

for, Jennifer. Allow yourself to grieve. I know how important it was for me to take time to experience the loss of my Gary."

I drew away from her, slowly. "Yes, of course." My throat tightened with remorse as I sought words, but came up empty.

"I'll check in with you in a bit, but you have my card. If anything comes up, any questions at all, please don't hesitate to call me. Okay?"

"Okay," I said, my voice sounding like a stranger's. "Okay," I said again, the second effort stronger.

Bernadette hesitated, then drew one of her business cards from her purse. She scribbled on the back of the card. "This is my personal cell phone number. You can call me anytime, Jen. Even if you just want to talk." She held the card out to me, and when I took it, she held it a moment longer, so that I would meet her gaze. "Anytime, and I mean it," she reiterated.

We walked back downstairs to the kitchen and out the back door. Louie and Francesca's cottage was situated on a slight hill in the back, and Louie's truck was gone. Bernadette and I ambled down the gravel driveway to where her car was parked in the front of the villa. I waved goodbye to her and turned back to my new home. Finally.

**

My footsteps echoed on the floor as I wandered in and out of the rooms. I'd been alone many times in our old house. For the last three years of our marriage, Jonathan had stayed in Washington most weekends, even when the Senate wasn't in session. He always had an excuse. And even when he was home, he'd schedule town hall meetings with constituents, have fundraising dinners at the Atwood Grille or the 1025 Club, events I wasn't expected to attend. He seemed more uncomfortable when I accompanied him. I stopped asking to go, and I think he was relieved.

The villa was situated in the small village of Gandria, just outside the city limits of Lugano. The lake was narrow at Gandria, and I could see over to the other side, where a couple of restaurants stood at the lake's edge. Bernadette had told me there was a tiny enclave, Campione d'Italia, farther down on the opposite side. It was Italy surrounded by Switzerland, she said. She didn't know much about its history, but said it had a casino, and when the boats operate, lots of tourists head there strictly to gamble away their euros and Swiss francs. The boats wouldn't be running until March or April, she'd said, so until then, if I needed to get to town, Louie would drive me. I found that I could walk along the lake and reach the Hotel Walter in under an hour. That was preferable to me. Louie seemed nice enough, though he had eyed me up and down with the corners of his mouth turned up. When he met my glare, he winked at me and licked his lower lip.

I was standing in the front room on the ground floor, lost in thought as I stared out at the lake, when I heard a gravelly voice behind me.

"Hello, Signora Logan." I whirled around to face a middle-aged woman who looked much older, her skin leathered by years in the sun, her voice like a torn burlap sack. Her hair was more gray than dull brown, and pulled back from her face, and her eyes drooped down at the outer corners. She looked worn out, exhausted by life.

"Francesca," I said, without the questioning inflection. I knew who she was. She remained with her arms by her side, so I resisted offering her my hand. Perhaps they didn't do that here. Louie had seemed a little put off when I shook hands with him. "Hello."

Her English was not good, certainly not as good as Louie's. "You like eat?"

I looked at my watch. It was two in the afternoon, and the breakfast I'd had back at the hotel was still with me. I shook my head no. "Five o'clock would be fine, thank you. Not much, though, just some vegetables, maybe a little chicken." Would she understand that?

"Five," she said, pointing to her watch, then holding up a hand with fingers splayed. I nodded. *"Verdure? Carote? Melanzana?"*

Verdure? I didn't know what that was. *Carote* sounded like carrots. "Okay," I sighed. Whatever. It didn't matter on my first night. Tomorrow I would make a list of my preferences and show it to Louie.

"Okay." Francesca gave me a curt nod and walked away, to the back of the house where the kitchen stood. Ours could prove to be a challenging relationship. I did not need someone to cook vegetables for me. I was capable of putting together yogurt and fruit each morning. Croissants didn't require anything. Meals weren't important.

Jonathan had refused to eat during that final week. On Christmas Eve morning, Cedella, his caregiver, tried to give him pureed turkey and potato and he'd pushed the tray away with so much force that food went everywhere and she burst into tears. We cleaned it up together and I suggested she go home to be with her family. She agreed, eventually, but promised to come back in the morning on Christmas Day.

"You don't need to come tomorrow, Cedella, really," I recalled saying to her. "Be with your children." I knew she had a few kids, but she'd never spoken of about a husband or partner.

"Yes, Ms. Logan, but I will come anyway at ten to see Mr. Senator Logan." She always called him that, and I never corrected her. Even to his face, she would call Jonathan 'Mister Senator.' I'm sure he never corrected her, either. He probably found it adorable.

Perhaps it was my subconscious, but I forgot to call Cedella and tell her that Mister Senator was dead. When she rang our doorbell, I realized she'd made the drive across town, leaving her children on Christmas morning, for nothing. I opened the door and told her that Jonathan had died hours earlier, and that his body was already gone.

Her breath escaped in a low, painful hiss. As a brightly-colored balloon with a slow leak would deflate, Cedella deflated in front of me. I took her arm and brought her inside, where I insisted she sit while I made tea.

"On Christmas Day?" she'd asked in a whisper. "I am so sorry, Ms. Logan. How awful for you. He did not seem to be so close. I know the signs." She wiped tears from under her eyes and looked up at me, searching for an answer.

My mind raced to find the proper words. "Yes. But it's a blessing that he didn't suffer for long."

"That's true. Can I help? Can I do anything for you? I'm here now."

"I'm fine. Thank you, Cedella. Thank you for everything. My husband was very fond of you." As she wept on the sofa, I found my checkbook and wrote a check. A big one. Jonathan would have done the same, I was sure.

CHAPTER SEVEN

I learned that walking was important. Every day after breakfast, I'd set out along the *Sentiero Dell'Olivo*, the Olive Trail, toward Lugano. The delicate footpath, not easily seen or known about outside of the residents, passed lovely villas and small hotels nestled into the mountainside. On my way to Lugano, the lake was on my left. Some mornings were chilly, and the clouds stayed low, hugging the lake, with no sun to lift them. Oftentimes I paused to stare at the water. Some days it was steely-gray, with secrets hidden beneath its surface. Other days it was so blue it hurt my eyes. And there was no snow to deter me.

There were olive trees, of course, and benches, stone walls, small parks, tiny alleys. Everything was a treasure to explore. I loved the solitude, but after all, it was February. I'd likely stay away from the path in the heavy tourist months to come. Sometimes the pathway was only wide enough for one person, and I couldn't bear the thought of encountering someone. I'd come to think of the trail as mine.

Within an hour, I'd arrive in Lugano. I'd wander the streets, occasionally stopping into the one big department store in town. There was always something I needed, since I'd brought so little with me. A rain hat, shampoo, wine. I made a grocery list for Louie after that first night, using a small Italian-English dictionary to come up with the right words.

Red apples. *Mele rosse*. Banana. *Banana*. I smiled. Oranges. *Arance*. Yogurt. *Yogurt*. Coffee. *Caffè*. What else? No bread. I wrote the word 'bread' and crossed it out with a big X. *Zuppa di verdure*. I would explain this to Louie, just vegetable soup in the evenings. I would try to eat my main meal out of the villa each day. It didn't matter to me that Francesca didn't have a lot of cooking to do. She was also my housekeeper, even though I made my own bed and kept the bathroom clean. She did my laundry and washed the floors. I bought my own wine, as much as I wanted. There was no one to judge me.

February felt like April. Days were mild and mostly sunny. Crocuses and snowdrops pushed up out of the dirt, yellow and purple gems against a brown backdrop. I wondered what the gardens would look like in a month or two.

One rainy day, I opted out of the walk to Lugano, instead donning my raincoat and my new hat, one with a wide brim and made of a water-resistant material. I checked the mirror and adjusted the brim so I looked like Ingrid Bergman in that scene at the end of *Casablanca*.

I strolled the footpaths and watched water drip silvery tears from the olive tree branches. On my way back to the villa, I encountered a stranger. I walked right into him. I wasn't looking, and certainly wasn't expecting to bump into anyone. It was the first time I'd met another person along the path. There he was, a tall man in a black raincoat. It startled me so much I let out a small gasp.

"*Mi scusi,*" I mumbled, pressing my back against a high stone wall in order to let him pass without touching me.

His silvery hair was wet and clung to his head. He eyes, red-rimmed and also full of water, looked past me, but he didn't move. He stood to my side, his mouth working as if he wanted to speak, but no words came out.

"Are you all right?" I asked.

His head moved wildly, neither a nod nor a shake, and drops of water spilled from his hair. He blinked. "*Sono così triste,*" he choked out. *Triste.* Sad?

"*È morta mia moglie.*" He swiped at his eyes. I didn't understand what he had said. But I sensed he needed me to stand next to him, in the rain, until he was ready to move on. I wished I'd brought my umbrella, but he seemed oblivious to the rain. He turned his face to the leaden sky and let the drops splash onto his skin. I waited with him. A silver drop clung to the end of his long, narrow nose before splashing to the ground. He shook his fist at the heavens and, in reply, they dropped more water on him.

"*Sei sposato?*" I still didn't understand him and shook my head. "I don't speak Italian, I'm sorry."

This man, as old as Jonathan had been, reached out and brushed his fingers against my wet cheek. It was as intimate a gesture as I'd felt in years, and I trembled like the leaves in the storm. I was unable to move. "Are you married?" he asked, and thunder rolled above us. I shook my head.

"*Un uomo sarebbe fortunato ad averti,*" he said in a voice as soft as a cloud. "*Niente è per sempre.*" And with the saddest smile I'd ever seen, he walked away from me, into the narrow cobblestone alley that led up the hill to the olive grove. I stood where I was and watched his back until he was gone.

**

There was mail for me when I returned to the villa in the afternoon. It was from Nancy, of course, the only person who knew where I was living. A large manila envelope was propped up, waiting for me on the tall marble-topped table in the front entryway, next to a white ceramic vase filled with pink tulips. Francesca. I smiled. We'd gotten used to each other, somewhat. She had coffee brewed for me each morning when I rose (six-thirty, every day — I am a creature of habit), and fresh fruit and yogurt available in the refrigerator, but she was always gone by the time I padded downstairs for breakfast. I'd pour a cup and bring it to the front of the house, where I could sit in front of the tall window and stare at the lake, if it wasn't obscured by low-hanging clouds and fog.

The morning quiet was a gift. I didn't have to make conversation with anyone, as I'd had to during my two weeks at the Walter. Remembering the kindness of the Eichers, I made a mental note to contact Lucia. I'd written a thank-you note the day after I'd settled into the villa, but weeks had gone by and I knew I should reach out in person. Should I invite them all to the house for dinner? She had told me they'd be opening the hotel in mid-March, so if I didn't do it soon, they wouldn't have the time to get away. I knew my obligations, and I was a good hostess. Francesca would cook for me. There was plenty of room for the five of them.

But first, the mail. The heat was on in the house, and it was cozy enough not to need a sweater. I poured a glass of wine in the kitchen and brought my goblet into the front room, where I lowered myself into a comfortable chair and slit open the envelope carefully with my key. There were six items within, including a note from Nancy:

Dear Jennifer, I hope you're acclimating to your new environment. I miss you! Life is different, as you can imagine, but I'm very busy and grateful for the job. I think of you often, and hope the villa is everything you'd hoped it would be. The professor who lives in your house contacted me, and I picked up the mail last week. He said he'd be happy to forward your mail, but I told him I'd be by every two weeks to pick up whatever might accumulate. He seems very happy in the house. Do you recall speaking with a man named Robert at the funeral? He telephoned looking for you and the call was directed to me from a different office. He said he was an old friend and was very sorry about the senator, but I haven't given him your whereabouts or any other information. If you want me to, just let me know. Anyway, I hope you're well. Send me a postcard from paradise. Fondly, Nancy

I folded her note and tucked it back into the envelope. Robert. Robbie. He would have identified himself as Robert, of course. Only I ever called him Robbie. At first I thought I had imagined seeing him at the funeral, through my Xanax-induced haze, but now I had confirmation that he was there. There was no reception afterward — I'd insisted against it — but during the procession out of the church, I'd lifted my head once we were outside and before I slipped into the limousine. Initially, I thought he was a hallucination. It was just as well we didn't have a chance to speak to each other. What was there to say? I'd made my decision years ago, first to leave him and then to marry Jonathan. Two choices I couldn't reverse.

The rest of the mail was nonsense. A fundraiser invitation from the Nugents, addressed to Sen. and Mrs. Logan, probably by a clueless intern who never read the news. A few sympathy cards from people whose names didn't register with me but who nevertheless wrote how wonderful my husband was and what a loss for the state and the country. I set them aside to throw away.

The rain had ended, but heavy clouds persisted, and the lake was gunmetal gray. I turned my eyes skyward and saw the same color reflected above. I'd had my walk, and the incident with the stranger was still fresh in my memory. I was glad to be inside for the rest of the evening. And I was hungry.

But Francesca had been instructed, explicitly, that I was fine and didn't need anyone preparing meals for me. My stomach protested as I wandered back to the kitchen and opened the refrigerator. And smiled. There was plenty of food. A cooked breast of chicken wrapped in plastic wrap that I took out and set on the counter. A glass bowl with a red lid. Lifting the top, I sniffed the contents. Twisty macaroni with olives and a creamy lemon sauce. Perfect. There was no microwave oven in the house — apparently Francesca the purist cook abhored them — so I turned the oven to low and let it heat up while I opened a bottle of white Merlot.

**

People back home used to tell me I was so lucky. Two women in the book club I'd joined and the guy in the deli that carried good lox, all three reminded me I was lucky to be married to such a caring, wonderful man. Our neighbor Melvin was the same age as Jonathan, minus three days. One summer afternoon we stood at the fence, each of us with a bottle in beer in hand. Melvin offered a toast to Jonathan, "the best senator this damn state's ever seen."

"I'm the lucky guy," my husband shot back. "Why did this beauty ever agree to marry me?"

Melvin shook his head and said, "Damned if I know, Senator." And we'd laugh, Jonathan with a witty comeback about getting it right the second time around, his hand on the small of my back, or gripping my shoulder a little too tightly as he steered me back into the house. Paula in the book club ('Literary Ladies of the East Side') had the temerity to ask how we'd met. I always hated that question, even if it was innocuous. When I thought back to our early days together, I could still remember him as charming and attentive. Me, having recently moved out of the loft Robbie and I shared, bunking in with one of the waitresses from work until I could figure out what to do next. Jonathan, smitten, generous, and a way to financial security that Robbie couldn't and wouldn't provide. I married Jonathan out of fear. I was scared to death of being poor all my life.

I always answered them with the same line: "We met in Boston, in a restaurant." I didn't say that I was a hostess, moved out front because I looked good enough for the high-end eatery. I didn't say that Jonathan blustered in with his buddy, also divorced. I didn't tell anyone how it began, in the back seat of a taxi, then in the Ambassador Suite of The Four Seasons Hotel. "We met in Boston," I'd say. "Lucky you," they'd murmur back.

Jonathan came from a long-established family with roots in Providence that went back to the time of Moses Brown, one of the founders of the Ivy League university in Providence. By the time we met, though, his parents were dead, his siblings were dead, and there wasn't anyone in the family left to condescend to his marrying me. A senator should be married, it seemed, and we didn't waste any time on courtship. Within three months of our initial meeting at the Black Orchid, we were engaged. Two weeks later we wed in front of his old friend Judge Peter Wetherbee. His daughter did not attend the wedding, citing plans that couldn't be changed. I believed her, of course. I didn't know her then, and Jonathan always spoke about Deirdre in the most positive terms.

"You two will get along, I know it," he told me one Sunday morning, early in our marriage. He was home for the long weekend but planned to fly back to Washington on Monday afternoon. We'd spent Saturday shopping for a new bed, at my insistence. Saturday night we dined at Providence's newest restaurant, where the small steak was over forty dollars and didn't include potato or vegetable. I never saw my husband pay a bill at a restaurant, so whether he had an account with the manager or someone else paid for our meals, I couldn't say. All I knew was that dinner with drinks and wine must have cost well over three hundred dollars. We took a taxi back up the hill to our house, and someone must have driven our car home, because it was in the driveway when I looked out the window on Sunday morning. I never asked.

At least once a month we'd arrive home drunk and wobbly, giggling and toying with each other. Those were the early years. I would pleasure my husband since he was usually unable to perform. And I didn't mind. I'd agreed to the arrangement.

Lucky us.

CHAPTER EIGHT

I invited Jean-Michel and Lucia, and the three children, to the villa for dinner, after checking with Francesca and receiving assurance that she could prepare a meal for all six of us. She made suggestions, good ones, and I left the planning and execution to her. She knew what she was doing, after all. Lucia was excited to receive my handwritten note, and telephoned the villa the next day. It was the first time the telephone had rung since I'd arrived, and the sound was dissonant and unfamiliar, like a broken bell.

"Oh, Jennifer, thank you! How are you? Is everything good at the Villa del Sol?" Her chirpy voice and enthusiastic manner made me realize how quiet things had been since I'd left the hotel. Yes, I welcomed a more quiet existence, but her laughter was like balm on a sunburn.

"Everything is fine, thank you. *Grazie*." I still hadn't learned much Italian, so it was futile to try and impress her. "So, Francesca will make the meal. Is there anything you or Michel or your children can't or won't eat?" I knew kids could be picky, not that I'd ever seen evidence of it at the hotel — her children were remarkably well-behaved.

"Luca once had a bad reaction to shrimp, but that is the only issue. We are all looking forward to seeing you!"

I thanked her and hung up. Even a short conversation with someone as nice as Lucia could wear me out. It would require practice to interact with people, unless I intended to be a hermit for the next four months.

**

After a quick note to Francesca about the shrimp, I climbed the stairs to my bedroom. It was only three in the afternoon, and the light was still good. But I lay on my perfect bed and closed my eyes. Over a month in Lugano and I didn't feel any calmer. Every night, before I finally fell asleep, I relived my final days with Jonathan. Attempting to settle myself by thinking about Robbie did no good — it was as if every time I tried to picture his face, I saw my husband instead, lying in a hospital bed with his skin like crumpled paper. Jonathan had been felled by the diagnosis. I was surprised he hadn't fought harder. My husband was a man I'd expected to stay young and active into his eighties. Instead, he had surrendered. And as much as I wasn't always happy in our marriage, I did enjoy certain aspects of my life — the opportunities to do good in the community, the fact that I never worried about money. I wasn't a spender — he had to direct me to buy new clothes and shoes for events, but I luxuriated in the knowledge that I had *enough*. There would always be enough. And that was because of him. He took care of me, he stayed with me, even if he no longer loved me.

Renting the villa was the one time in my entire life that I spent more money than I was comfortable with. I know I could have leased a small apartment in town. I could have rented something a lot less grand and still have had a view of the lake. But I craved the feeling of space all around me. I hoped the solitude would calm my soul and assuage my anxiety. I wanted to feel as placid as the glassy lake. I wanted to be as free as the whispering breezes that would soon blow warm on my face. There was so much space that I didn't know what to do with it. I skittered around the empty rooms with abandon. I twirled on my toes, my arms above my head, because I knew no one would see me. I sang in the bath, I climbed the stairs over and over again for exercise. I loved being by myself, but I would welcome the Eicher family into my temporary home. Having five more people in the dining room would fill the long rectangular table.

**

Francesca buzzed around the kitchen like a

deliriously happy gnat. She hummed, she sang, a solo with unintelligible lyrics to a song I didn't recognize. I stayed out of her way and fidgeted in the living room. I straightened pillows that were perfectly aligned, I checked spotless windows for fingerprints. I changed my clothes from too dressy to too casual to ran-out-of-time-this-will-have-to-do slacks and a sweater.

When the front doorbell chimed, I felt my heart leap toward my throat. There they were, all five of them, gathered on the wide front steps. Lucia held a bouquet of pastels.

"Welcome!" I said, opening the door for them to enter. I watched their faces as they stepped inside — the boys slack-jawed, Isabella unimpressed by the grandeur. Michel stole a quick glance at his wife, then spoke.

"Jennifer, it's grand! Are you comfortable here?"

"I am, yes. I do enjoy the space, but I don't use it all, of course. Come, sit. I'll let Francesca know you've arrived." I hurried back to the kitchen and found her placing drinks on a tray.

"Oh, thank you, Francesca. You didn't have to do that."

"For the children," she murmured. Orange juice and a fizzy beverage called Rivella, as well as San Pellegrino water. "You eat in twenty minutes." She raised her eyebrows in question.

"Wonderful, thank you. Would you like to meet my friends? See the children?"

Clouds passed over Francesca's eyes for just a moment. She shook her head no. "I finish here, then I go." She turned away from me and busied herself with nothing. I picked up the tray.

"*Mille grazie*," I said, wondering what heartache was part of her life. Didn't we all have something?

**

The meal was superb, everyone agreed. Francesca must have kept the children in mind when she created a not-too-sophisticated menu. We started with classic bruschetta, oven-toasted bread slices topped with plum tomatoes, basil, garlic, and fresh mozzarella drizzled with a balsamic vinegar glaze. A bowl filled with greens, cucumbers, tomatoes, olives, capers, and feta cheese stood ready for family-style serving. Francesca plated thick-cut pork chops and topped them with parmesan-gorgonzola butter before handing the platter off to me. I brought it, along with a large shallow bowl of garlic mashed potatoes, to the table as I heard the back door close. Our feast ended with individual tiramisu, six glass goblets layered with sponge cake, mascarpone, and chocolate. Three of the goblets were marked with a paper that said '*Adulti – cognac.*'

As we enjoyed coffee, Luca asked if they could go to the top floor.

"No, Luca, that is not polite," Lucia said.

"It's okay," I countered. "I don't mind. They might like the view from the top floor. Okay?" I looked to Michel and Lucia for approval, then directed them to the back staircase off the kitchen. After they had left and we heard them stomping up the wooden stairs, I leaned back in my chair, full and happy.

"You have wonderful children."

Michel suppressed a grin. "Thank you, Jennifer. They're not angels, you know. Lucia can confirm."

"Of course not. They're kids. But they're beautiful and mannered. You've both done very well."

Lucia nodded when I offered cognac from the bottle Francesca had used for the tiramisu. I sensed she didn't have a chance to relax much, and it was good to see Michel withhold his own alcohol intake so she could indulge.

"Did you want to have children, Jennifer?" Lucia asked. I saw Michel touch his wife's hand. "Oh, I should not ask? I'm sorry."

"No, it's all right." I turned my eyes to Michel. "Really, it's all right. When I married my husband, I knew he didn't want children." I wasn't sure how much they knew. Had Bernadette told them? "My husband was much older than I, and he has a daughter — Deirdre — who is actually older than I am." It still made me laugh, the absurdity of it all.

"It's not unusual, not in Italy anyway," Lucia said. "Men take wives, mistresses, have children everywhere..." She let her sentence trail off and sipped her coffee. "I could tell you stories."

Michel deftly changed the subject. "You know that my mother came from Rhode Island?"

"Yes! Yes, she told me. Although I understand she hasn't been back in some time. It's probably changed since she was there."

"She has a sister who lives there. They all came to visit last summer. Do you have any brothers or sisters?"

It was all very...nice, I thought. All this pleasant conversation. But through all the civility there were probing questions. Too many for me.

I pushed my chair back and stood. "No, I was an only child," I said. "Would either of you like more coffee?"

Michel wasn't stupid, nor was he tipsy like his wife. He stood as well. "No, thank you. I believe we should get the children home. Shall I head upstairs to get them?" Without waiting for an answer, he bypassed me and strode into the kitchen. I heard him climbing the stairs and calling out for his kids.

Lucia looked as if she could fall asleep at the table. I picked up cups and saucers and the bottle of cognac on my way to the kitchen. I would do the dishes after they left. It was the least I could do, not to leave everything for Francesca.

Michel reappeared, with his boys in tow and Isabella in his arms. At six, she was still treated like a two-year-old, in my opinion. It wouldn't serve her well in the future, I thought with some bitterness. No one had ever coddled me, that was for sure.

"Why don't you bring the car up the driveway to the back door?" I said. "It will make it easier. I should have suggested it earlier."

"Oh, but that entrance is something," he said, smiling. "Jennifer, thank you for a most enjoyable evening. It was very gracious of you, and please tell your cook that she outdid herself."

"She'll be pleased to hear it. I'm glad you all liked it." I reached up to stroke Isabella's curls, and she turned her sleepy face into her father's chest.

"You know, we'll just leave the way we came in. Let me make sure my wife hasn't fallen asleep."

I remained in the kitchen while they gathered themselves, and listened to the murmurs and protestations of one sleepy child and one inebriated wife.

As they made their way out the front door, down the steps to the car, I watched the boys take their mother's elbows to guide her down the stairs, as Michel balanced Isabella. This wasn't something I would ever have, I thought. It didn't bother me at that moment, although I was well aware that in twenty years, I might feel very differently.

CHAPTER NINE

The day I met Donnalee Dunwood was the fourth day of March. March fourth, the only day on the calendar that was also a command. Jonathan used to tell that joke at fundraisers and the whole room would erupt in laughter. Donnalee was standing outside, perched next to a table at the entrance of my favorite café, the place I'd become comfortable enough to stop in every other day for a meal and a glass of wine. It was early afternoon, the sun was playing hide-and-seek with big puffy clouds, and I had decided to sit outside under a cheery red umbrella emblazoned with the word 'Cynar,' which I understood was an Italian liqueur made from artichokes. Yellow daffodils, pink and red tulips popped out of concrete planters that stood guard at the doors to banks, offices, and restaurants. Sunlight, when it was present, sparkled on the lake and I took my seat with a direct view through the cars and across the street to the blue majesty of Lake Lugano.

Donnalee stood out among the conservatively-dressed Swiss in a red-and-white-striped sundress. A thin white cardigan was draped recklessly across her bare shoulders. My first thought was that the first week of March was too early for summer clothes. She didn't seem to notice that it wasn't hot out. Her shiny black hair was cut short and severe like that girl Amélie in the movie, and red earrings bounced against her long white neck as she talked and laughed with two men who were seated at the table. She was animated and loud, and American. I cringed inwardly — why do Americans have to draw so much attention to themselves? Why do they perpetuate the myth that we're all loud and obnoxious? Well, she wasn't being obnoxious. The men seemed drawn to her, and as I sat at my table, with a plate of *tagliatelle al sugo* and a glass of Merlot, I couldn't take my eyes off her. Her angular beauty was softened by an air of indolence and languor.

What made someone so comfortable with themselves? One of the men at the table pulled out her chair, but she swatted him away, like a pesty fly, then she laughed and bent to kiss him. He must be her mate, I thought. He fixated on her like a puppy. The other man, wearing non-American clothes, sported a distinctly European metrosexual, androgynous look. He fidgeted constantly and his head swiveled on his neck as he looked around the café. As he set his stare on me, I realized that I had been staring at the trio. I ducked my head and concentrated on my lunch.

I forced myself not to look at them for the rest of my meal, but the sound of a chair scraping the concrete deck had me raise my eyes and I found myself staring at the well-fitting trousers of the metrosexual.

"*Scusami,*" he said in a low, lovely voice. "*Sei bellissimo. Ma si è da soli.*" His lips curled up and he tilted his head toward his left shoulder. Although he had pulled the chair out, he remained standing behind it. His meticulously-manicured and unadorned hands rested on the chair's back.

I set down my glass. "I don't speak Italian," I said evenly, lifting my eyes to his face. He had long eyelashes and neatly-groomed brows. I made a mental note to book a salon appointment. If he was trying to pick me up, I wasn't interested. I knew '*scusami*' and I figured out '*bellissimo.*' "Sorry," I added and turned back to my meal.

"I'm sorry," he said. "I assumed you were Ticinese. My apologies, miss. Enjoy your meal."

I watched him retreat and rejoin his friends. He spoke to the pair and the woman pivoted to look at me with curious eyes. She raised a hand and fluttered her fingers, then grinned broadly. Oh dear. I've been discovered by the American, I thought. I gave a cursory nod in return, a small smile, and summoned the waiter for my check.

But I couldn't escape them. She flung off her cardigan and tossed it on the empty chair. With her mate close behind her and the other man trailing at a respectable distance, she approached me.

"Hi! I'm Donnalee Dunwood. My friend Fulvio here tells me you're American." She cast a sidelong flirty glance in Fulvio's direction. "At least he said you *sound* American. Are you?" She pulled out the chair across from me and sat down, uninvited. The waiter came by to remove my plate.

"Could we get a bottle of whatever wine she's having?" The waiter nodded and left. "What's your name?"

"Jennifer," I said. No use in lying. She extended her hand across the table like a debutante, fingers together pointing downward. I couldn't shake her hand, I could only hold the fingers. I noticed her nails were polished shiny red and imagined she changed her nail polish as often as she changed her outfits.

"Well, Jennifer, it's nice to meet you! I could use a girlfriend. This is my fiancé, Rodney. He's a teacher at the Tasis. And you met Fulvio. Guys, come on, sit." She spread her arms like Jesus as she motioned to her friends, who seated themselves in the other two chairs at the table.

"Nice to meet you...all," I said. I was trapped at my table, and Donnalee had just ordered wine. How do animals react when they know they're trapped? They can be vicious. I wasn't a vicious person, but I was certainly trapped. "What is Tasis?" I directed my question at Rodney, but Donnalee answered.

"It stands for The American School in Switzerland. It's the oldest American boarding school in Europe, you know. Rodney teaches English. The students all adore him." She raised her shoulder and dipped her chin while giving him a look that I'd seen in the movies, mostly in satirical comedies. It was the same look she'd given Fulvio.

"And what do you do, Donna?" I knew she'd start asking me questions, but I figured I could stave it off by asking her about herself, a topic which I assumed she'd be all too happy to explain.

"It's actually Donnalee. All one word. Don't worry, everyone makes the same mistake." She pursed her red lips. "What do I do? I do a little translation here and there. I make sure my babes is happy when he comes home. You know, play wife." She winked at Rodney. "We're getting married in June." She held out her left hand, palm down, to let me see her ring. It looked more like a cocktail ring, with a large rectangular light blue stone surrounded by diamonds, possibly, or cubic zirconia. It didn't matter to me, of course – and it seemed to suit Donnalee perfectly.

"Lovely," I murmured as the bottle of wine arrived. The waiter set glasses in front of us and poured four even servings, which emptied the bottle. I would limit myself to this one glass. I turned again to Rodney, wondering if was capable of speaking for himself. "Do you not have school today, Rodney?" I smiled at him, encouraging the man to answer.

With a glance at his bride-to-be, Rodney shook his head. "Not on Fridays," he said. He had a wet way of talking, as if there was too much saliva in his mouth all the time, and I wondered if Donnalee was embarrassed by it. Maybe that was why she answered for him.

"So, Jennifer, let's have your story now. Why are you here?" Donnalee rested her chin in her palms, her elbows on the table, eager to hear my tale. She would be gloriously disappointed in the truth.

I smiled and slipped my hands under the table, where I held them tightly together in my lap. My nails dug into my palms. "I'm widowed recently, and simply came here for some peace."

"*Niente è per sempre,*" Fulvio murmured, and I looked up sharply. That's what the old man had said when I met him on the Olive Trail in the pouring rain.

"What does that mean?" I demanded.

He looked up at the sharpness in my voice, and seemed surprised, as though I'd scolded him. "Nothing is forever," he said. "I'm sorry, I meant no offense." His dark eyes looked like pools of melted chocolate. And those lashes. I felt a flutter in my chest and shook it away.

"No, you're right. Nothing is forever. *Niente è per sempre.* I'll remember the phrase now." I watched as the others drank wine. No one seemed to notice that I left my glass untouched.

**

Donnalee's voice had tiny bells inside it. They tinkled when she laughed, which was often, even when it wasn't appropriate. Her lilting cadence and slight, south of the Mason-Dixon line accent were lovely when she kept her voice down, but this was a woman who needed to be heard, all the time. Rodney hung on her every word, never taking his eyes off her, but I sensed Fulvio staring at me.

"What did your husband do?" I expected Donnalee to return to talking about herself, and her wedding plans, rather than ask me more questions. After I said I was widowed and came to Lugano for peace and quiet, I'd have thought that would be enough for most people. She leaned across the table and lowered her voice to a loud whisper. "How did he die? If you don't mind my asking."

I did mind, of course. And now there were three pairs of eyes trained on me, waiting for a sensational revelation about Jonathan and his last days. I was young, so they assumed my husband was young, too. I sat up straighter in my chair.

"My husband was in politics," I said, my fingertips brushing imaginary crumbs from the white linen tablecloth. "He had cancer." I looked up, at each of them in turn, first Rodney, then Fulvio, and finally Donnalee directly across from me. "He didn't suffer. And that's all I'm going to say. If you don't mind."

Donnalee drew back, her black-rimmed eyes wide. She swallowed hard before gulping down the wine in her glass. Perhaps she'd never faced death, never lost a loved one. It was possible. She was young, too, younger than I.

"I'm so sorry, Jennifer. That's just awful. We won't talk about it anymore." She patted the table, ending the topic for all. "Now. Why don't we eat something?" And without waiting for me to say that I'd just finished a meal, she raised her small white hand, with the red fingernails and the giant blue ring, and summoned our waiter.

**

Donnalee gave me her telephone number and made me promise to call her. That was how I avoided having to give her my number. There was a telephone at the villa, of course, the telephone that never rang. But she was stubbornly persistent, and I did have to tell her where I lived. As long as Francesca was in the house during the day, mopping the floors and doing the laundry, she could be my buffer against uninvited visitors. When I returned home that afternoon, I made sure to tell her, and used Louie as my translator to ensure she understood.

"I don't want anyone coming to the house uninvited, do you understand?"

"Yes, of course, miz, but we cannot stop them from approaching the door," Louie countered.

"Right," I said with a sigh. "But they are not to be allowed inside. And you must never say that I am home. Say that I am out, and be sure to get a name."

They both nodded their understanding. It would be just like Donnalee to show up, with Rodney and Fulvio in tow, either to peek inside the villa or try to drag me out of it. I knew it wasn't possible to hide from the world, and in truth, it wasn't that I wanted to necessarily. I enjoyed watching people interact. But I wanted it to be on my terms.

For all the years I was married to Jonathan, networking with strangers had been on his terms, at his direction. I attended fundraisers and social events with him, when invited. I lifted a glass of warm chablis as another sycophant stood, slightly drunk, to make a sodden toast to him. I did all the things that were expected of me, and tried to dispel the rumors that I was nothing more than a trophy wife. I even sent an anonymous letter to the state's treasurer, offering a complex solution to the state's fiscal crisis. They implemented a couple of my suggestions, and I never revealed that I had sent the letter. I really didn't want the publicity, and I knew there would be plenty of snarky comments, anyway. People who knew nothing about me assumed I was an airhead.

When a week had passed and I hadn't phoned Donnalee, I hoped that she would have moved on and forgotten about me. No such luck. On a beautiful Saturday morning, with the tall windows open for fresh air, and with Francesca humming in the kitchen, I heard a car drive up. Its occupants were loud (well, one of them was) and spoke English. I was upstairs in my bedroom looking for a hair clip when I heard the doorbell ring. Its melody echoed throughout the house, and sounded like glass wind chimes in a breeze. I stood still, listening for Francesca to answer the door, praying she would remember my instructions.

I tiptoed to the landing to listen, and smiled. She spoke only Italian, not even attempting any English after Donnalee introduced herself and asked if I was home. I heard Donnalee's voice loud and clear.

"Jen – ni - fer! She does live here, yes? Fulvio, would you speak to her, please? She doesn't understand."

Fulvio then rattled off something in rapid Italian, and I listened for Francesca's voice. I checked my watch. She worked until eleven on Saturdays, and was off all day on Sunday. It was ten-thirty. Perhaps she was weighing her options.

Then I heard the big door close and Francesca's footsteps on the marble floor. I inched closer to the staircase and peered down. She was on the bottom step, looking up at me.

"Are they gone? *Partito*?" I whispered. She held up her index finger, then, with the same finger, motioned for me to come downstairs. I crept down the stairs in my socks, almost laughing out loud at the absurdity of sneaking around in my own residence to avoid people who might or might not be outside. But the windows were open, and I wasn't sure if they were really gone. I followed Francesca to the west side of the villa, to a window overlooking the gardens and pool. She held that same finger to her lips and pointed.

There they were, speaking to Louie, who was working in the garden. The window that looked out on the gardens was shut, so all I could hear was muffled voices, mostly Donnalee's. I watched her arms flutter in animation as she flirted with Louie. He glanced back at the window where we were standing, and I quickly stepped away, out of sight.

After a few minutes, I heard the car's engine roar to life as they made their noisy departure, back toward Lugano. I rolled my eyes at Francesca and she gave me a rare smile.

"You no like these people," she said. A statement rather than a question. I shrugged.

"They're okay. She's loud. I don't like people coming here without an invitation."

"*Non invitato*," Francesca said and I repeated the phrase. "*Non invitato*."

"*Sgradito*," Francesca added, and when I looked at her questioningly, she translated. "Unwelcome."

"Absolutely. *Sgradito. Grazie*, Francesca." But I knew they'd be back. And I couldn't hide from people forever.

CHAPTER TEN

As spring gained its ground and the blooms took over, life around the lake increased, too. There were more people about, strolling past the villa on the footpath that hugged the lake shore, many stopping to admire the structure. The villa, modeled after the Villa Balbianello on Lake Como, was smaller than its mentor. The Balbianello stood where there once had been a Franciscan monastery. My villa had a *campanile*, or bell tower, but Louie, who gave me the detailed history of both the Balbianello and the Del Sol, told me there were never any bells in the bell tower of the Del Sol. Louie and Francesca had worked for the villa's owner for years, and although he was discreet about some aspects of his employer's life, Louie liked to talk. He believed he could impress me with his tales.

I learned much about Vittorio Guttuso, the villa's owner. Louie brought me a newspaper, from years back, and pointed to a photograph on the front page. It showed a man with white hair climbing out of a limousine.

"This is Signore Guttuso," he said. His index finger stabbed the photo. "Very famous."

"Really," I said, feigning interest.

"*Si*. Famous but not for good reason," he added, and raised his bushy eyebrows for emphasis.

"Is Signore Guttuso a criminal, Louie?" It pained me that I immediately thought of the Mafia, but I'd lived in Boston and Rhode Island long enough to understand how things worked.

Louie used his fingers to form an 'X' in front of his closed mouth, a gesture I didn't understand. With his hands and his eyes, he conveyed thoughts and sentences. It was almost laughable.

"Okay, I don't need to know. As long as I can live here until the end of July, I don't care what he does."

"He travels. I have only met him three times, miz." He indicated three with his thumb, index finger, and middle finger. "But Francesca and me, we are paid to keep everything, yes, nice. Nice."

"Yes, everything is very nice, and thank you, Louie. *Grazie*."

**

I continued walking the Olive Trail, more for exercise than for anything else. I never again saw the old man I'd encountered on that rainy day, but I thought of him often as I walked. How bereft he was at the loss of his wife. Did I miss Jonathan? Of course I did. When I found out that he was sick, sitting next to him in the doctor's office as the doctor announced his diagnosis and desperate prognosis, I held my husband's hand. He would need me, finally. He couldn't handle it alone, I knew that. He knew he could trust me. In our eight years of marriage, I had never betrayed him, never spoken out of line, even when I was angry with him. A couple of hours later, back home and alone in our house, we made love with a ferocity I hadn't seen in him since the early months of our marriage, when he was insatiable. I understood. He needed to be virile, to be strong, and I went along with it all. I loved him with sincerity, caressed him gently, held him as he sobbed. It was probably the closest we'd ever been. He poured his heart out to me like the sea, in passionate wave upon wave, and I was a sponge.

"No one can know about this illness, Jen," he'd said, his lips right on top of mine. "No one. I'm not going to fade away like some old...."

I touched my fingertips to his temple. "You know I'll protect you. At every turn. You don't look sick, darling. You look as strong and healthy as ever."

His eyes, still wet and shiny, looked deep into mine. He trusted me. And I wouldn't let him down.

There would be no chemo. Dr. Epstein had advocated for treatment; my husband was just as adamant in his refusal. He flew back to Washington on Sunday evening, following an afternoon spent watching football. I'd made a pot of chili, his favorite, and we sat close together on the sofa, with our feet propped up on an ottoman wide enough for four. When I returned from the kitchen after cleaning up, he was typing into his cell phone.

"What's up?" I asked.

He glanced up from his phone, turned it off, and smiled. "Nothing," he said. "Just letting Dan know which flight I'd be on." Dan was Daniel Westover, the junior senator who adored Jonathan. Neither of us stated the obvious — that Dan would soon be the senior senator from the great state of Rhode Island.

"Don't you two always take the same flight?"

"Hmm? Oh, yeah, usually. Just confirming." He stretched and rose from the couch. "Gonna get my things together, hon." He pecked my cheek and made his way upstairs.

I stood in the living room, staring at his phone, face down on the side table. I so wanted to check it. Had he really texted Dan? Or someone else? My husband's past transgressions gave me plenty of reasons to doubt his story. I took a step toward the phone. Did I want to know? Would he run to another woman in DC, and sob in her arms, too? Would he love her with all the strength and energy he had with me?

The phone vibrated. All I had to do was turn it over. I took another step. I'd always respected his privacy, even when I was sure he'd been cheating. I knew there were women — he'd slipped up more than once. I knew. And still I stayed.

"Jen? C'mere for a sec," he called down the stairs. With one last glance at the phone, I turned and made my way upstairs.

CHAPTER ELEVEN

Bernadette telephoned me a day after I received a lovely note from Lucia. It was late March, but spring had definitely arrived. Of course, in Rhode Island and the Northeast, spring sometimes brought snow, but in Lugano, the temperature was warm, flowers were in full bloom, and the boats plied the lake from morning until sunset.

I picked up the phone and was surprised that I felt so happy to hear from her. After avoiding Donnalee and her two hangers-on for the past couple of weeks, with success, I was full of nervous energy.

"Jennifer! I hope I haven't called at a bad time," she said. It startled me to hear her unaccented English, as all I'd been listening to the past few weeks was Italian or English with a pronounced Italian accent. Bernadette spoke without the whiny nasality of the typical Rhode Islander. Her enunciation was very good, probably from speaking English to so many foreigners, I imagined.

"It's good to hear from you," I said, meaning it. "How kind of you to phone me."

"Well, I did want to give you time to settle in. How

are you doing?"

"I'm fine, thanks. Each day brings something new. But I've become accustomed to the villa, and I'm enjoying the spring. It's as if the calendar is a month or two ahead of what I'm accustomed to."

She chuckled. "You know there's still skiing? The mountains still have plenty of snow. My husband is in Zweisimmen now." She paused, then added, "I don't ski, and besides, I'm too busy setting up summer rentals."

The hills around Lugano were devoid of any snow, and that was fine with me. "It's really lovely here," I said. "How's everything with you?"

She cleared her throat. "Good, good. Listen, I have some work down your way. I'd really love to see you, Jennifer. Any chance we could meet up?"

"Of course," I replied. I liked Bernadette, probably more than anyone else I'd met. "Would you like to have dinner here? Do you need a place to stay?" Listen to me, I thought, all hostessy and inviting. But it was Bernadette. I wouldn't mind her company.

"Thank you, really. That's so nice! But I'll be staying with the kids. I can't very well come to Lugano and not stay with them! They always want to give me a room for free, but I insisted on paying. Michael offered me a senior discount! Can you stand it? How about lunch? Next Tuesday? Would that work for you?"

I almost laughed. She must know I never had plans. My schedule was as wide open as the lake. "Next Tuesday is great. What time?"

"Could you meet me at the boat launch at ten? Is that too early? I know a sweet little spot down the lake. We could have a stroll around before lunch."

"Sounds like an adventure. Sure, I'll see you there at ten." And before I hung up I added, "Thank you."

"Looking forward to it!" Bernadette sang into the phone before she disconnected.

I hadn't yet taken a boat ride on the lake, but I would see them slide past occasionally, when I was at my window. There was a stop in Gandria, a short walk from the villa.

Other than the long, unplanned trip to Bern that I took when I was still staying at the hotel, the only other journey I'd made was a short train trip to Locarno, which was situated at the northern tip of Lago Maggiore, north of Lugano. My guidebook told me that Locarno was about one-fifth the size of Lugano, by population. There was a church high above the city, and since I was there for the day, I took a funicular up the hill to Orselina. I passed people, modern-day pilgrims, hiking up the steep and narrow footpath to the church. They used rough-hewn walking sticks and carried packs on their backs. The funicular inched to the summit where the massive ochre structure, perched on a steep, rugged rock, dominated the area. The views from the portico in front were spectacular, and I could have sat under the overhang and simply contemplated the view of the lake below. But the sanctuary waited behind me, so I stepped into the church.

And drew in a sharp breath. Never had I seen such a display of opulent magnificence. Frescoes, stuccoes, canvases. Every single item on display was there to pay homage. It all shouted at me until I found a place to sit. Then the quiet enveloped me. There were only three other visitors inside the church — an elderly couple who spoke in reverent whispers as they passed me, and a woman with a pronounced limp who walked with care toward the front altar, where she knelt on one knee for twenty minutes. I stayed in the back and tilted my face to the domed ceiling. Baroque paintings on a cobalt background filled the space above me. My mind's swirling chaos quelled, as if by a holy calming hand.

**

Donnalee had telephoned twice, and eventually I had to call her back. I hadn't made a phone call in months. I didn't miss the telephone at all; a strange statement from me, since my phone had been like an appendage before I married Jonathan. Back then, I couldn't imagine being without it — it was my watch, my camera, my dictionary, my meteorologist. But in Lugano, I didn't miss it. There was a flat-screen television in my bedroom, but I'd only turned it on a couple of times. I couldn't understand the news in Italian, or German, and even after I'd discovered the BBC channel, it didn't interest me.

"Hey, you!" she chirped when I identified myself to her. "Where have you been hiding?" A gentle sarcasm snaked through her voice.

"I'm sorry," I said automatically. "I've been traveling a bit. How did you get my number?"

"Oh, Jen, I can find anything! And you know, you can call me any time, I don't mind. I sleep with my phone under my pillow. Always getting texts," she added.

"That must make it hard to sleep through the night, though."

She laughed. "Yes, it sure does! But I'm addicted to my phone. Hey, are you free, like this afternoon?"

A quiver of resistance ran through me, but I knew I couldn't dodge her forever. "It depends on what you've got in mind," I replied, sounding coyer than I'd intended.

"I'm heading to the Marbella," she said, referring to the café she frequented. "Please say you'll come. I could use a friend. A *girl*friend."

Donnalee wasn't the kind of woman I'd consider a girlfriend, but she was the only woman I knew here. Well, there was Bernadette, but she lived in Bern, and Lucia was busy with the hotel and her kids. "Okay, sure. Just let me change my clothes. I'll see you in an hour?"

"An hour? I'll be half a bottle in by then," she said, sounding delighted with the prospect.

"Well, I was going to walk," I trailed off. I listened to the silence on the other end, and I thought I heard a faint sniffle. "Never mind, I'll get a taxi."

"Yay!" she said and clicked off.

The Marbella was crowded, mostly with tourists, and I spied a big bus with *Hafermann Reisen* painted on the side. Donnalee had already ordered food, and there was a nearly-empty bottle of white wine on the table. I ordered a San Pellegrino.

"You're not drinking? Oh, Jen, I hate to drink alone." She made a little pout, an expression I guessed worked well with Rodney. But considering the fact that she had managed to drink most of a bottle before I arrived, I assumed she really was just fine drinking alone.

"Not today," I said breezily. "I'm putting on weight. Too much pasta."

"You look fine, are you kidding me? *I'm* the one who should be dieting, but I just love eating and drinking so much!" She scooped up the last of her risotto, and poured the rest of the wine into her glass. "Here, eat some bread. I can't." She pushed a cloth-covered basket in front of me.

When the waitress approached our table, Donnalee ordered for me. I noticed she never attempted to speak Italian. "The risotto was fabulous. She's having San Pellegrino. And a salad."

"Caesar," I said. "*Per favore.*"

**

As I ate, Donnalee looked around the café. "Now, who's here?" she muttered.

There was always someone she knew, it seemed, and sure enough, I'd just started chewing when she called out. "Santiago! Over here!" She waved with an exaggerated gesture, like she was up in the bleachers or a half-mile away. In a stage whisper, she said, "He's the partner of Milo, who teaches with my Rodney." Santiago was a handsome man of about thirty, tall, with thick black hair. His large dark eyes were wide-set, his lips were perfect and full, and he had that scruffy unshaven look that women seemed to love.

"*Bellissima*," he crooned as he bent down to kiss Donnalee's cheeks. As he straightened up, Donnalee winked at me and said, "Sant, this is my new friend Jennifer. She's *American*, and was married to a United States *senator*, but now she's a *widow*." Through all of the overdisclosure, Donnalee made three distinct faces for her friend — 'be impressed' for "American." 'Be more impressed' for "United States senator," and finally, 'be very sad' for "she's a widow." It was like watching a bad actress in a worse sitcom. I extended my hand in greeting and said, "Nice to meet you. I'm the widow."

Donnalee erupted in laughter and slapped my forearm. "You kill me, Jen!"

"Hello," Santiago said. "I'm very sorry that you are a widow. You are too young, too beautiful." I didn't know whether he was being kind or flirty. I chose to think he was kind, since Donnalee had mentioned his partner was a man named Milo. I thanked him.

"Sit down, Sant," Donnalee said, her voice mushy from the wine. Turning more to me, she added, "Did I tell you Sant's partner works with my Rodney?"

"Yes, you did." *My Rodney?* Could she not say his

name without underlining the fact that he was hers? I wasn't interested in him, and Santiago already had someone.

"Oh!" Donnalee snapped her fingers. Her face lit up like a switch had been thrown, with a thousand volts of electricity directed at her smile. "Jennifer, you should throw a party! You have the perfect place! Sant, Jennifer lives in the Villa del Sol. Do you know the place? Over in Gandria?"

Did everyone know about the Villa del Sol?

Apparently Santiago did. "That's a very beautiful place," he said. "Just you in the big villa?" He sighed deeply, perhaps with envy, perhaps from exhaustion.

"Just me, yes. I like a lot of space." That wasn't even true anymore. I thought I did, but I'd been wandering the rooms, listening to my footsteps reverberate against the walls and ceiling. Sometimes I would sing just to hear a human voice. I'd begun talking to myself when I knew I was alone; otherwise Francesca would think I'd lost it completely.

"Let me think about it," I said. I was dimly mistrustful of the idea, and of Donnalee, too. But perhaps a party was what I needed. I knew how to throw a good party.

"Okay, missy, but you know it's a great idea!" She wiggled a finger at me and asked Santiago to order more wine.

I was about to leave when Milo and Rodney strolled in, and then I had to stay. I hadn't met Milo, so introductions were made, more wine was ordered, and the men perused menus. I didn't want anything else to eat and my bottle of San Pellegrino was empty. I asked for a pot of tea when the waitress returned to take orders.

"Jennifer isn't drinking today," Donnalee whined to the table. I shrugged it off and turned my attention to Rodney, who was seated on my left.

"Your day ends at a reasonable hour," I said. "Do you start early?"

"Depends," he replied. "Today was more of a half-day. I have a long day of classes on Tuesday, and I teach an evening course as well. So it's usually not worth going home in between. I stick around, have something to eat. Sometimes Dee meets me afterwards..." He trailed off, and I caught the furtive look he shot her way. She didn't see it, though; her attention was focused on Milo and Santiago.

"Did you always want to teach?" I asked him, hoping to keep our chat going. Donnalee was acting as if Rodney wasn't even present. I wondered if she did that on purpose. It certainly kept him close and attentive. He responded to my questions, but I could tell he was also listening in on the other conversation.

"Yeah. My mom was a teacher, my dad was a high school principal. That's how they met. Back in Maryland, I taught high school English, but the kids didn't appreciate Hemingway or Orwell. Or Willa Cather, no matter how much I tried." He leaned back as the waitress placed a steaming plate of truffle pasta in front of him. "I wanted to travel, so I got trained in teaching English as a Second Language. Less than a year later, I was able to snag a temporary spot at the Monte Rosa." He took his first bite and tilted his head back in pleasure. Donnalee had left the table and gone to the bar. Her torso bent toward one of the men there as she chatted and fluttered, and the man seemed enraptured by her every word.

"I'm not familiar with Monte Rosa," I said, glancing first at Donnalee, then at Rodney, who squirmed in his chair. He, too, had seen her at the bar.

"It's a private boarding school in Montreux. Quite well-known," he added, then, seeing my face, added, "Well-known to those of us in the profession, that is. No one else is familiar with it, either. Want some of this?" He held out his fork, and a long strand of fettucine curled around it, glistening with creamy sauce. "Come on, it's good!"

I took the bite he offered, and savored its velvety saltiness. Then I caught Donnalee staring at me. Her bright eyes, like a hawk's, were unblinking, her red lips parted as if ready to snatch a mouse in her teeth. I looked away.

"Still," Rodney continued, "the kids there liked me, the staff did as well, and one of the senior advisors recommended me for the position at TASIS." I noticed that Rodney's 'wet' way of speaking wasn't evident in this conversation, and I wondered if it was his fiancée's presence that produced the excessive saliva in his mouth.

"Okay, people, we leave now," Santiago said as he and Milo stood. "Nice to be meeting you, Jennifer." I shook hands with Sant and with Milo and then it was just Rodney and me at the large table. Donnalee, in spite of the hard look she had fixed on me earlier, was still at the bar, now with her back to us. If she was concerned about me being alone with her Rodney, she made no move to intervene.

"How did you meet Donnalee?" I questioned.

A quick cloud passed over his face and was gone. "She was at a business conference in Zurich." He pushed more pasta into his mouth, glanced again at his fiancée holding court at the bar, and looked back at me, blinking rapidly. There was silence between us as he chewed and swallowed.

"Actually, that's a lie. It's what we tell people, but I'm tired of lying. She was in Zurich, but as the girlfriend of someone I knew, one of my teaching colleagues. We were attracted to each other right away, I mean, look at her, right? She told me they were just friends, there was nothing serious between them." He picked up his glass but set it down without drinking. Then he pushed his empty plate across the table, away from him. "Well, they weren't just friends. I didn't know that, honest. I screwed over my buddy." He tapped his finger on the table next to his wine glass.

I wasn't sure what to say. "But you didn't do it on purpose. You didn't know."

"No, I didn't, really. I believed her. And maybe that was how she saw their relationship. She thought they were just friends, he thought more of it. But they were together." He glanced in her direction again, and she had turned. He caught her eye, and she blew kisses his way. "I'd never known anyone like her. No woman had ever wanted me so much, had ever devoted herself completely to me the way she does."

I thought about the fact that she'd cheated on her former boyfriend to be with Rodney. I wondered if it was part of her nature. Once a cheater, always a cheater? I had some knowledge about that. But my role was listener, not advisor. I already knew more about these two people than I wanted to know.

"How are the wedding plans coming along?" Change the topic, I told myself. On to happier subjects.

Rodney brought his glass of wine closer. He let out a short bark of a laugh. "We argued about that today. We're supposed to get married in June, here, and now she wants to postpone it. What woman wants to postpone her wedding?" He waited for me to answer. His gaze searched my face for an appropriate response, but I had none. His eyes were full of unconquerable hopefulness.

When I didn't answer, he continued. "Sorry, was that a sexist remark? I didn't mean it that way. Now she's saying she thinks a Christmas wedding would be nice. I don't know if she's just buying time."

"Well, Christmas is a lovely time for a wedding. And if that's what Donnalee wants, it does require a little more time to plan. Would you get married here, or in the States?"

"Well, that's the thing," he said, refilling his glass and placing the now-empty bottle back on the white tablecloth. These people drank wine like it was water, I thought, watching him for signs of inebriation. His speech was clear, though. "Here, we would just do it, get the marriage license, have the ceremony, a small party afterward. But if she's set on Christmas, then we'd fly back to the States, have it in Philadelphia with both families. Ugh. That's not the way I'd envisioned it. We had agreed on something small, more Swiss."

I smiled at that. Understated like the Swiss, I got it. Three months in, and I understood exactly what he meant. "I'm sure it'll all work out," I said, the lamest comeback I had in my arsenal.

**

Donnalee, like a magnet, pulled herself back to us, waving goodbye to her entourage at the bar. "Jennifer, let's definitely have a party at your villa! It's the perfect place for it! We stopped by for an impromptu visit recently, but you weren't home." Donnalee's sad face. "Your caretaker is so lovely and charming and he said it wouldn't be a problem. So let's make a date!" Donnalee's extremely happy face.

I took a taxi home. It was late. My impromptu afternoon meet-up with Donnalee had transitioned into an hours-long fest. The last boat had left Lugano an hour earlier and I didn't want to walk the dark Olive Trail by myself. Lugano and its area were quite safe, certainly safer than Providence, but why put myself through the forty-minute walk? The trail was only dimly lit in spots. I had reluctantly agreed to the party, realizing it was nearly impossible to say no to Donnalee, and rationalizing that I needed to be more social.

CHAPTER TWELVE

I met Bernadette as planned, on Tuesday at ten in the morning at the boat dock. The clouds were high and scuttling fast in a blazing blue sky, and there were more cloud banks behind every hill and mountain. We were still a couple of weeks shy of full-out tourist season, so the boat wasn't crowded — only a couple dressed in mountain hiking clothes who spoke German loudly, a businessman who never once looked up from his phone, and two teenage girls who stared at the businessman and giggled.

Bernadette grasped my hand as we boarded. "I'm so happy to see you, Jennifer! You look wonderful. Villa life agrees with you, I think." She slipped a pair of sunglasses on, and I couldn't see her pretty green eyes anymore. "Tell me how you've been doing."

I had to admit that villa life did agree with me. "I've gotten into a good routine here. Most mornings I walk into town along the Olive Trail, forty minutes, thirty if I power walk, which I rarely do! I'm eating well, maybe too much pasta, but it's so good." I didn't mention the sleepless nights. They weren't every night, and what difference would it make? I knew why I wasn't sleeping.

"You're working through your grief. I know the routine. Good for you."

Was I working through my grief? I'd been in Switzerland for less than three months. It was three months and three days since Jonathan had died. I expected it would take longer for a spouse to 'work through' grief, but I wasn't like other spouses. There were still moments, of course. And in those sleepless nights, I relived the final hours, the last time I looked into his eyes, his words to me, his grip on my hand before I left him. I'd throw aside the covers, fling open the balcony doors, and gulp air that was cold and uncaring. I'd stare into the blackness, where it was impossible to see where the water ended and the land began. I'd listen to the eerie quiet – no motors, no animals, no screams.

Our boat, named the *Milano*, pulled away from Lugano and rumbled toward Paradiso, its first stop. As we passed near the *jet d'eau*, similar to but smaller than the well-known fountain in the middle of Lake Geneva, the breeze shifted and I felt the spray on my face. It was good, and then it evaporated in the caress of soft sunshine. A metallic voice over an intercom announced our stop at Paradiso, where we waited just seconds before moving on.

Bernadette pointed out Monte San Salvatore, and said I should make a plan to go up to the summit. "Wait a month or two for warmer weather, but it's worth it, Jennifer. Take the funicular from Paradiso, then there's another five-minute walk to the very top. When the clouds aren't low, your view is spectacular, so just plan it for a clear day." I made a mental note.

She turned to face me. "Is everything working out with Louie and Francesca? I know Francesca can be…mercurial."

"No, they're both great," I said. True, Francesca was fickle in nature, some days almost pleasant, other days gloomy and dark, but she did her job well. She balanced Louie's effusive personality, and I guessed they evened each other, too. How else could a marriage like theirs work so well for so long? "Francesca and I are making our way through the language."

Bernadette laughed. "Are you learning Italian? *Parli italiano?*"

"Unfortunately, not so much. I can understand a menu, but I don't have much chance to learn. I don't watch television, and if I want to read a newspaper, I pick up the *Times* or *USA Today* in town. If I want to know what's going on at home. Which I usually don't."

"But Jennifer, you don't want to close yourself off completely." Bernie leaned in closer. "I'm sorry. It's not for me to say. Forgive me, that was uncalled for."

125

"It's all right. Actually, I've met a couple of Americans here. An actual couple. She's...very outgoing, I guess that's how I should describe her," I stammered. I didn't mention the party that I'd agreed to host. There wasn't a clause in my rental agreement or anything saying I couldn't host a party. It was more that I didn't want to disappoint Bernadette, or even have her question my motives. Like I needed her approval, which was crazy. She wasn't my mother.

"I was going to suggest Lucia for Italian lessons, but she's so stretched out with the hotel open now. If I asked her, she'd say yes, but I know she doesn't have time."

"It's all right. I'll make more of an effort to learn."

The boat made a quick stop at Melide, and Bernadette mentioned there was a wonderful little miniature village that I had to see sometime (another mental note). Then we arrived at Morcote. The beauty of it caught in my throat.

"See the church? That's Maria del Sasso."

I interrupted her. "Maria del Sasso? I was in Locarno recently and there's a church of Maria del Sasso there as well. Bigger. High up above the lake."

"You're thinking of the *Madonna* del Sasso, above Locarno. Yes, the sanctuary. This is the church of *Maria* del Sasso, probably five or six hundred years old. *Sasso* means 'rock' in Italian. Both churches are built on rock."

Ah. *Sasso*.

"Morcote de-stresses me like no other place I know," Bernadette said dreamily. She led the way off the boat. "You know, Michael first saw Lucia here."

"Really?"

"Yes, he was interning at Walter at the time. Isn't it interesting that he now owns the hotel where he began his career? And she was on vacation with her parents." Bernadette pointed to a restaurant situated right upon the lake, it seemed. "There. Ristorante della Posta. That's where they first met! He was smitten."

We strolled through the piazza, and I felt the benevolent warmth of the sun on my face. "Were you smitten when you first met your husband?" I asked.

"Gary? My first husband?" Bernadette smiled, and her eyes skimmed across the lake to a far-off place. "No, not smitten," she said. "I wasn't smitten with Gary. He was a college friend, but it wasn't until many years later that we found each other." Her chin lifted and her lips curled upwards, but it was as if she was speaking to herself. Tenderness breathed from her with every word. "Gary was such a good man." She touched a fingertip to the corner of her eye. "They don't come along often." She turned and gave me a bright smile. "Come on, let's find our restaurant. You can tell me all about meeting *your* husband."

**

Over gnocchi with basil and grilled lake perch, we talked about Rhode Island and our shared knowledge of the city of Providence. I would mention what had changed and Bernadette knew about a lot of it, claiming that her sister's emails kept her up to date.

"So, did your sister tell you about my husband?" When I first arrived in Switzerland, I'd assumed that Bernadette knew about Jonathan's political status, and his death. I figured the owner of the rental agency, Nancy's friend, would have filled her in. After all, it was juicy gossip, the elderly senator, much loved and revered, his much younger wife, now a widow. Maybe Bernadette's sister had sent her links to all the salacious stories. I'd seen enough of them in the ten days after his death. I couldn't wait to fly away from that place.

"Only in passing, Jennifer. I never discuss my clients with anyone. My sister Joanie doesn't know that we're acquainted. Just as you'll never know who else I represent." She smiled and plucked a breadstick from a slender glass cylinder on the table. She twirled it like a baton, and when she looked up to see me smiling at her, she broke into a grin. "I've still got it, forty years later!"

I liked her. She was the real deal. Someone who respected another person's privacy was all right with me.

"I could stay here all day and drink wine with you," I said. We'd already killed a bottle of Bianco di Merlot, a white Merlot that went down easily. But I hesitated to suggest we order another bottle. After all, it was early afternoon, and I didn't want Bernadette to think badly of me. Again, I was worried about her disapproval. "Not that I would!"

"Maybe some coffee instead?" she asked. I nodded.

**

We walked around Morcote and I purchased a small copper sun to hang on the wall at the Villa del Sol. When our boat pulled up to the dock, we boarded and found seats away from the bright afternoon glare. A shimmer of golden sun shook through the trees along the lake's shore. I dozed in the shade as the boat made its lazy way around the lake. My copper sun, wrapped in brown paper, slept inside the big straw bag that rested at my feet. When I opened my eyes, Bernadette was leaning against the railing of the boat, making sharp hand gestures as she spoke into her phone. Probably her husband. She hadn't talked as much about her current husband as she had about Gary, the one who'd died. Gary was obviously the love of her life. Is first love always that way? Maybe. I never felt for Jonathan what I'd felt for Robbie. Jonathan was my protector, sometimes my detractor. He provided me with financial security, and maybe it was the same for Bernadette. Being married to Gerard allowed her to stay in Switzerland, and she could be close to her son and grandchildren.

She returned to sit next to me. "Sorry," she apologized. "Had to check in with Gerard." She glanced down at her watch. "I think I'm going to stay another night. We won't arrive back in Lugano until five-thirty. I wouldn't get home until ten."

"Please stay at the villa!" It came out so fast, I surprised myself. I didn't want her to leave. "You know there's room. Where's your car?"

Bernadette pulled at her hair, twisting one corkscrew around her finger, as she considered my rushed-out invitation.

"Please?!"

"Sure, why not!" She squeezed my hand. "We'll have a slumber party." She grinned at me and I felt as though I was a wave on a happy sea.

The day sang itself into the soft glow of evening. Over more Merlot and lasagna that Francesca presented (I think she brought over what she had made for herself and Louie, since I never ate much at night and suddenly I asked for supper), Bernadette told me the story of her son. She always called him Michael, not Jean-Michel, not Michel. Michael. Her unplanned pregnancy while a college student in Fribourg. Her almost-abortion in Paris, the people who helped her through the year. Her father's sudden death.

"How did you find him, your son?"

She explained about her searches, and candidly told me about how it had affected her professional career and life.

"You used to be a lawyer? Right in Providence? Wow," I said. I knew a few lawyers, through Jonathan, and we had a family attorney who I didn't much care for. Of course, back when Bernadette was practicing, I was still in diapers. It was unlikely that she'd know the people I knew.

Bernadette laughed lightly. "No wow. I drank too much, got fired from a good job with a good firm. I slept around, led a very unhealthy life. I was obsessed with finding Michael. I never needed to worry, as it turned out — he was always safe, always happy. It was only after I forgave myself that I was able to function like a normal human being. Finding my son, and falling in love with Gary, were the greatest blessings of my life."

I thought about that. "But you live here now. Are you still in touch with your friends? What about Michael's father?"

Bernadette sighed. She lifted the empty bottle and raised her eyebrows. I nodded and pulled another from the wooden rack next to the table. My brain was fuzzy around the edges, but I didn't care. I poured more wine for both of us.

"Well, Jen, I'm nearly sixty years old. Many of the people I knew way back when are gone now. Michael's adoptive parents have passed, Bruno first, then Klara. Karl Berset, Michael's birth father, died a few years ago." She paused in thought before looking up. "He had Huntington's. Fortunately, Michael did not inherit it. One of Karl's other children did, though, his son, and the poor boy took his life because of it. He just couldn't face his future."

"How awful," I said.

"Yes. He was filled with despair. He knew he would meet the same fate as his father, and he couldn't live with it."

I could imagine. The boy had been handed a death sentence in advance. "What about the woman who took you to Paris when you were pregnant? When you…?"

She shook her head. "When I didn't know if I could go through with it," she finished my question. "I'm not sure. Erika was a free spirit." With a smile, she added, "Wherever she is, I'm sure she's happy."

I wanted to know more. "The doctor? Hanna? It sounds like she was a good friend to you."

"She was, and she is. Hanna and I are still friends. We get together a few times a year."

I marveled at her story, and at her courage. I wanted her to keep talking.

"Jennifer, I've told you enough for a book. Your turn, girlfriend. Spill your guts. Tell me about your friends in Providence. Better yet, tell me some secrets." Bernadette's head bobbed as if her neck was a metal spring.

The wine couldn't be trusted. Or, I couldn't be trusted with the wine. Or, whatever. I was sober enough to realize that I was at that edge, and I knew to choose my words carefully. I was good at keeping secrets, and I wasn't one of those people who felt better after confessing everything, like the guests on Oprah or Dr.

Phil.

"What do you want to know?"

"Tell me about the day you met your husband," she encouraged. I'd cleared the table and brought the dishes to the sink, where they soaked in soapy water. We moved to sit at opposite ends of a long sofa, my bare feet tucked under me, Bernadette's propped on a low table in front of us. We faced the French doors that led onto my balcony. The indefinable yearning for days that were long dead wrapped around me.

"It was night, not day," I began. "I worked in a restaurant in Boston. I started as a waitress, and then was moved to hostess," I added, looking for a reaction.

"Well, you're gorgeous, I bet he noticed you right away."

I didn't acknowledge the compliment. Comments about my looks grated on me. It was just genetics, that was all. Genes don't determine what kind of person you'll be. But Bernadette was right. It was the way I looked that got me put out front and caught Jonathan's eye.

"He'd been divorced for years. His ex-wife and daughter had moved to California. He was...lonely." Horny, I silently corrected myself. Denying the years, his age. I made him feel so young, he'd sing to me, sounding nothing like Sinatra.

"Was he schmitten?" Bernadette laughed at her slipup.

"Sure, he was smitten. With everything from the neck down."

"Come on! You have a pretty face!" She laughed. "But we know men, they're looking at all the other stuff."

"Yeah. He didn't think I had anything between my ears." She squinted at me and I was emboldened. "I'm smart, you know, Bernadette."

"Call me Bernie. I hate it but all my friends call me Bernie."

"You hate your name?"

"I hate it! I wish I'd been named Jennifer." At that I laughed out loud. Bernie turned on me.

"What? How'd you like to go through life as a Bernie?"

I leaned back against the sofa and waited. "What?" she asked again.

"I wasn't Jennifer when I was born. My mother

named me Farrah."

"Farrah? Are you kidding?"

Now it was my turn. "Do I sound like I'm kidding? Farrah. As in Farrah Fawcett. Charlie's Angels."

"Oh, my God," Bernie sputtered.

The memory of humiliating years roared back to life. "Just as you hated Bernie, I hated Farrah. I changed my name when I turned eighteen."

"Really? What about your parents? Were they mad?"

If she wanted truth, I would need more wine. I poured the last of the bottle into my glass. "I never knew my father," I said softly. "And I don't know if my mother was mad. I didn't see her much around that time, and by the time I did see her again, I was already Jennifer. But she still called me Farrah."

Bernie sat silently on the couch. I was just getting started.

"I never went to college. There was no money for it. I worked, usually more than one job. I lived with friends for a couple of months at a time, until I knew I wasn't welcome anymore. Then I met someone." In spite of my intoxication, I didn't want to talk about Robbie. "And then I waitressed, until I was moved up front at the restaurant." I glanced over at Bernie. She was watching me closely and biting her lower lip. "My husband wanted a young wife, someone to show off to his friends, to prove he could still get the girl. No, it's true. Come on, he was thirty-seven years older than me. Everyone called me a gold-digger, one woman even said it to my face. But they said nothing against *him*."

"So why'd you marry him?" Bernie's voice was nearly a whisper.

"Money," I said flatly, looking straight at Bernie. She stared back at me, then burst out laughing.

"Sister!" She held up her open palm, waiting for me to slap it.

CHAPTER THIRTEEN

I hadn't expected to like Bernie so much, especially as I was closer in age to her daughter-in-law, but we clicked and it felt good to have a girlfriend. Donnalee was not going to be my girlfriend.

The next morning, we ate breakfast together and drank a lot of coffee. I apologized to Francesca for leaving dirty dishes in the sink and she waved me away.

"Is okay," she said. "Anything else?"

"No, *grazie*," I said.

"I drank a lot more than usual," Bernie said after Francesca had left. She tore off a piece of croissant and peered into the white ceramic pot that was filled with apricot jam. "Do you have any chocolate?"

"I'm sure there's some here. You like it with the croissant?" I opened a cupboard in the kitchen and found a bar of milk chocolate studded with slivered almonds. I handed it to her. "Help yourself."

Bernie tore open the wrapper and broke off a large piece, then sliced open her croissant and slid the chocolate inside.

"I eat chocolate every day, usually in the morning." She lifted a shoulder before taking a bite. "Good. Hey, did we end up drinking two bottles of wine?"

I nodded. "That was a lot for me, too. I feel it this morning. Sorry!"

"Don't apologize. I had a great time." She looked up. "My husband doesn't drink at all. By choice. He's a health nut," she added, rolling her eyes. "So I don't usually drink around him. Which is fine, probably even better for me." She shrugged. "It was nice to feel so comfortable with you last night that I let loose."

"Well, I'm glad you stayed. I hope I didn't run my mouth all night." Truth be told, I couldn't remember how much I'd told her.

Bernie giggled. "You think I remember?"

The French doors were open, and I inhaled the pristine freshness of spring. My secret would remain a secret.

As we finished our breakfast, I shifted in my chair. "I agreed, reluctantly, to host a party here in a couple of weeks. I checked my rental agreement and it doesn't say anywhere that I can't. Maybe you could come?"

Bernie swallowed before speaking. "You can have a party. How many people?"

I laughed. "I only know a couple. But they know people. Not too many, I hope." I'd have to check with Donnalee. I hadn't thought to ask, but twelve seemed like plenty. "Why don't you and your husband come?" I tried to sound casual, like it didn't matter either way.

"In a couple of weeks, I'll be joining Gerard in Nice. He's competing in an endurance event and I'm along for the ride." She must have sensed my disappointment. "But I can't wait to come back and visit!" She pulled a lipstick from her purse and applied color without even looking in a mirror. "Gotta fly, Jen. I want to check in with the kids before I head back."

"Do you want aspirin?" I should have asked earlier, when we first got up. Now it was as if I was just trying to keep her in the house. Or at least that was how I saw it.

"All set, my friend." She gave me a brief hug and I determined to break free first. Smiling my senator's wife smile, I walked her to the door.

"Must have rained overnight," Bernie said as she stepped outside onto the stone piazza. She inhaled deeply. "Ah, I'll never grow tired of clean Swiss air! *Ciao*, Jen."

"*Ciao*, Bernie," I called, watching her drive away.

I returned to the living room, and now the house was filled with an awful quietude. I knew I needed to host the party.

**

For the dinner party, there would be eight of us. Me, Donnalee, Rodney, their friend Fulvio. Rodney's colleagues at the school Lily and her boyfriend Claude, Milo and his partner Santiago. I'd asked Louie and Francesca. Louie seemed pleased, Francesca didn't. Although I never could read her poker face.

Francesca and I worked on the menu together and finally agreed on buffet-style. I did not want her serving people. I hated the way it looked, and I knew most of Donnalee's friends were socialists. Francesca was not a maid, anyway. I think she appreciated my logic, at least I hope she did. We decided on easy foods for guests to pick up at their leisure. No plated dinners. Sit, stand, drink, eat. Repeat as needed.

I helped Francesca clean for the party, even though the ground floor was immaculate. We could have put the food directly on the marble floor. I knew my guests would want a tour of the villa, even if I tried to confine them to the ground level. Americans always want the tour, always want to see your bedroom. So we cleaned upstairs, too. Fresh linens, fresh towels, fresh flowers everywhere. Louie shopped from my grocery list, and brought back two cases of wine in the bed of his pickup truck. Forty-eight additional bottles of wine, on top of the ten or twelve already in the house. My guests could drink all they wanted, although I'd be sticking to fizzy water. I needed to be sharp; after all, this was not my house, I didn't know the other people, and I wasn't about to let anyone trash the place. Besides, I knew Donnalee and her friends were big drinkers.

Francesca and Louie set up the food an hour before anyone arrived. She had special plates that plugged in to keep cold food cold and hot food hot.

"Francesca, thank you for all of this. I never expected to have a party here, and it's been a lot of extra work for you. *Grazie*."

"*Prego*," she said, moving a stray lock of hair away from her eyes. "*Divertitevi*. It looks very nice." She gave me a small smile.

"Will you stay for the party?" I touched her forearm. "Please?" Again, I was begging someone to stay.

"No, no. I like a quiet time," she replied. "I come back to take away the food." Again she gave me a tired smile and turned away. Francesca was a woman of few words, even in Italian. I'd witnessed her with Louie and they conversed using looks and hand gestures more than words. No small talk between them. I liked that. There were times when I'd say banal things to Jonathan in a futile effort to start a conversation. It usually didn't work — my husband could stand up on the floor of the United States Senate and talk forever about tax incentives, clean water action, gun restrictions, but when he was with me there was nothing. I knew about legislation, I knew what he was passionate about. Perhaps by the time he came home to me he was all talked out. Meanwhile, I stooped under the sheer weight of loneliness. Sometimes the silence between us was almost ominous. Had we already exhausted every topic in just eight years?

My guests arrived in two cars. There was one extra, a young woman who was introduced to me as Trina, Donnalee's hair stylist. She sported a nose ring and multiple tattoos and eyed me suspiciously. The rest of them entered the villa roaring and flashing like a glittering army.

"I invited Trina to come along, Jennifer. I knew you wouldn't mind one more, and Fulvio needs someone!" Donnalee didn't wait for me to react; she grabbed a glass and filled it, then linked her arm through Rodney's and wandered to the tall windows.

The food stayed mostly untouched for the first two hours, and, even with the cold and hot plates, I worried about someone getting food poisoning from food that hadn't been kept hot or cold enough. At the two-hour mark, I collected eleven empty wine bottles and brought them to the kitchen, where I rinsed them and deposited them back into their plastic crates. Francesca was gone, having said a quiet *'ciao'* to me an hour earlier. She reminded me that she would be back around midnight. I wondered if my guests would be gone by then. They were drinking a lot, and I couldn't let anyone drive while intoxicated.

I stuck to my promise and consumed only sparkling water as I watched everyone around me get drunk. I tried to push food into them. Lily, a tiny-waisted Asian woman with sleek black hair, made a small plate of fruit and cheese and set up a slightly larger plate for her companion. Rodney ate more than anyone else, but he was also drinking faster than anyone.

I noticed Louie moving quietly through the house and nabbed him near the ornate staircase.

"Everything okay, Louie? Is Francesca okay?"

"*Si, si*, everything okay. She sleep now, come back later." I smelled wine on his breath as he spoke. Well, he was an invited guest, so what did it matter?

"Okay, *grazie*," I said, heading upstairs. Just a quick check to make sure no one was using my bed.

Two hours later, the food had been cleared away and refrigerated. I'd have leftovers for days. I collected four more bottles — fifteen in total, some half-filled, but I was to find more empties the next morning.

Every single person in my house was too inebriated to operate a car and I didn't have enough beds for everyone. It didn't seem to matter, as the party wore down. People simply passed out in chairs and on sofas.

Someone played music off a cell phone — a slow instrumental, and Donnalee swayed close against Louie. His hand rested on her lower back and she nuzzled his cheek. I looked away. There was Rodney, a glass of red wine in his hand, staring at his fiancée. I assumed he was passed out if Donnalee was dancing with Louie. No one else was awake. I sat down next to him, avoiding the bodies of Fulvio and Trina intertwined on the rug.

"Hey," I whispered. "You all right?"

"She's like the sun," he said. "She enters a room, and she's the sun. Everyone wants to be in her light."

We watched Donnalee and Louie move together, as a couple would, and I wondered why Rodney didn't get up to separate them. It didn't have to be confrontational, but why wouldn't he take her gently by the arm and bring her back to him? Rodney finished what was in his glass and looked around for another bottle. I gently took the glass from his hand.

"Maybe if you call it a night, she will, too," I suggested.

Rodney's eyelids were heavy, but he was afraid to fall asleep, I could tell. I didn't know how long they'd been dancing, but Rodney was going to wait them out. And just as I thought he might give up, Donnalee and Louie moved imperceptibly away from us and toward the side door, which was open for some cool night air. They headed outside toward the pool. I wanted Rodney to pass out. Please don't see this, Rodney. Please don't do this, Donnalee.

**

Dawn crept in from the lake like a guilty child. I was awake, listening to the still quiet. I rose from my bed and dressed quickly, anxious to survey the damage in the morning light. I was determined to clean up before Francesca came in and discovered it.

Bodies were everywhere. Thankfully no one had tried to drive. Trina, Donnalee's goth stylist, was sprawled across Fulvio on the bed in the first guest bedroom. I guess they'd found their way upstairs from the rug. They'd left the door open but I didn't recall hearing them. I stepped softly to the back bedroom and found Lily and Claude spooning in the bed, also with the door open. They both purred like kittens. So that took care of four of them. Five more. I climbed the back stairs to the third floor. There wasn't a bed on the top floor, just some exercise equipment. I stopped on the top step and listened. Nothing. Slowly, taking a step inside the cavernous space, I squinted and spied Rodney, lying on his back, facing away from me, his hands locked behind his head. He was alone. My heart sank.

Where was Donnalee? I felt a surge of panic rise in my chest, into my throat where it turned into bile as I realized Donnalee might have spent the night with Louie. I wanted to find out before seeing Rodney, but as I turned to sneak back downstairs, I stepped on the creaky floorboard and gave away my presence. Rodney sat up quickly and turned around to face me.

"Hi," he said. "I thought you might be Dee." He stood, stretched, and walked toward me, his palms out and turned up.

"I'm sorry, Rodney. I haven't seen her. I just got up myself." After a pause, I added, "We all drank a lot last night." The first part was true — I hadn't seen Donnalee yet. The second part was true except for me.

"She's probably downstairs," he said, and I wondered if he believed himself.

"Why don't you let me put on a pot of coffee. You

can use my bathroom if you need to." I was trying to buy a few minutes' time, but I knew I wasn't fooling him. "I'm going to clean up."

"I'll help you."

Maybe it was better for him to face it.

"If you want."

"I should find Dee," he said. He slipped into his shoes and followed me down the two flights to the kitchen.

Francesca was already at the sink, washing dishes. I felt like a ten-year-old who had neglected her chores. Although, when I was ten, I took care of the house. My mother was either too drunk to function, or sleeping it off.

"Francesca, *mi dispiace*. I'm sorry. I got up early to do this so you wouldn't have to." She didn't turn around.

"Is okay. I work." Lifting her soapy hands out of the sinkful of water, she turned and asked, "You want breakfast now?"

I wanted everyone out of the house, that's what I wanted.

"Just coffee, please." Shit. I needed to wake

Donnalee and Louie. Didn't Francesca wonder where her husband was? And where had Rodney gone?

"Excuse me," I said, leaving the kitchen and the dishes and the crates of empty wine bottles.

I practically ran into the living room. Milo and Santiago were on the balcony, their arms around each other, waiting for the sun to slip above the mountains. I opened the side door and stepped outside, where I spotted Donnalee lying on a chaise by the pool, covered with a brown-and-orange blanket I didn't recognize. Rodney was seated beside her, gently pushing her hair from her forehead. Donnalee's eyes remained closed. So Louie wasn't with her? The relief I felt was palpable. Donnalee and Louie may have spent 'quality time' together by the pool the previous night, but at least he wasn't there now, in her arms. I wanted to know what had happened, and I didn't. It was the same way I'd acted in my marriage.

So everyone was accounted for. No one had stumbled down to the lake in the darkness and fallen in. Louie was likely in the cottage, sleeping it off. I wondered if Francesca put up with infidelities from him. Donnalee and Rodney hadn't yet acknowledged me, so I returned to the kitchen and asked Francesca to prepare a small buffet breakfast.

"I'll help you," I offered, setting fruit on a plate. Maybe if my guests drank coffee and ate some food, they'd be more inclined to leave. But what about the couple upstairs? I couldn't walk in and wake them. It was barely seven o'clock.

Francesca had paused and was eying me warily. "Everyone stay?" she asked.

I set my jaw. "They can eat, then they must leave." I searched my memory for the word, then remembered. "*Sgradito*."

Her eyes smiled back at me. "*Si*. Unwelcome."

CHAPTER FOURTEEN

A thought occurred. I would enlist Donnalee. It was the least she could do for me. I opened the side door and walked down a flagstone path to the patio.

"Good morning!" I called out in a chirpy voice. "Beautiful day!"

Rodney continued to stroke Donnalee's forehead as she covered her eyes with her hand.

"Ssh, Jennifer, not so loud," she whispered.

I was undeterred. Stepping closer, I said, "I hope you slept well! We have coffee and fruit and pastries for breakfast. And *Dee*?" I used Rodney's pet name for her and it got her attention. "I'll need your help in moving things along, you know, waking everyone up. I have an appointment later this morning and need to be out of the house."

She narrowed her eyes. "It's Sunday. What do you need to do on Sunday?"

I hesitated. "Church. It's Palm Sunday. Mass is at ten. Want to come with me?" I smiled big, and could tell she didn't know whether to believe me or not.

"Seriously? I didn't know you went to church." She sat up slowly, with Rodney's assistance.

"Ever since my husband died, I've found Mass to be very…healing." It was partly true. I had been afraid to go to church, imagining God might find a way to bar my entrance. But if Donnalee bought my story and got her friends out of the villa, I'd attend the morning service at Santa Teresa every Sunday.

"We'll take care of everything, Jennifer," Rodney promised, patting Donnalee's foot. He stood. "Let me fuel up first." He leaned down to kiss Donnalee on the mouth and I swear I saw her flinch. He left us alone on the concrete patio, with Donnalee still stretched out on the chaise and me standing over her, hands on my hips.

Once I heard the side door close, I turned on her. "Did you sleep with Louie?"

She yawned, without covering her mouth, and didn't answer. When she closed her eyes, her lashes were like tiny fans on her cheeks.

"I know you did."

"Then why are you asking?" Her dark eyes opened and blazed at me.

"You talked me into this stupid party. What a mistake," I muttered.

"Oh, Jennifer, relax. Everyone needs an opportunity to chill, you know. I've been so stressed out over wedding plans and everything. I drank a lot of wine, and Louie is very charming. We didn't have real sex, anyway. If a man did what I did, other guys would be clapping him on the back."

"That's ridiculous," I snapped, but wondered if Jonathan's old fat golf buddies, or that ham-faced senator from the Midwest, would have congratulated him for nailing another young woman in DC. I pictured the lot of them, married, divorced, rich and powerful, each trying to outdo the other, and my stomach turned.

I was relieved Bernadette hadn't been able to make it. How embarrassing it would have been. She was so much more of a friend than any of the pretenders taking up space in my villa. Too bad she lived so far away.

"Coffee's inside, Donnalee," I said. "Drink up, and get your friends the hell out of here."

**

With everyone 'fueled up' and gone by nine, I decided to honor my lie/promise and attend Mass.

On Palm Sunday, the churchgoers were dressed in

colors as vivid and lively as a spring garden — fuchsia, lilac, chartreuse. A large woman in a blindingly yellow dress took her place in the pew in front of me. Sitting behind her was like staring directly at the sun.

I was raised Catholic by my grandfather, who insisted to my mother that 'the girl needs a proper religious upbringing.' Pop lived a couple of streets away, with his wife, who was not my mom's mother. He'd wait for me to come out of school when I was six, seven, eight, and he'd walk home with me, then he'd give me two Chips Ahoy cookies and a cup of milk. He made sure I ate, made sure I was clean, had clean clothes to wear, and he took me to church every Sunday. On the rare occasion my mother was able to function as a mother, he'd step back and let her.

When I was almost nine, Pop went to the hospital and never came home. His wife, whose name was Violet, walked me home from school three more times before informing me that she was moving to Florida. My ninth birthday came and went without a party or a cake. My mom slept the whole day and the next one, too. A week later I walked home from school by myself and used my key to open the door that led into the kitchen. My mother and Albert were sitting at the table, waiting for me.

There was a cake with white frosting that said 'Happy Birthday Farah,' and I wondered if my mom had forgotten that my name had two Rs in it. She handed me a plastic Wal-Mart bag and said, "Honey, you know I can't wrap for shit."

I reached inside the bag and pulled out a bright yellow sweatshirt with a Tweety Bird on it. It had a small hole at the neck and was really big, an adult size XXL. When they insisted that I try it on, it came down past my knees.

"See? It can be a nightgown until you grow into it!" All I knew was that I never wanted to grow into it.

"You're already starting to blossom," Albert said, as his eyes raked my body.

After we ate cake — I had the last of the milk, Albert and my mom each had a beer — I said thank you and lied that I had a book report due the next day. I took my sweatshirt to my bedroom and folded it into the bottom drawer of my dresser.

The large woman in the bright yellow dress stood and waved to someone.

I clasped my hands in my lap and waited for Mass to begin. It was all in Italian, but I remembered the words to the prayers in English.

Nel nome del Padre, e del Figlio, e dello Spirito Santo. In the name of the Father, and the Son, and the

Holy Spirit.

And later, *Padre nostro, che Sei nei cieli.* Our Father, who art in Heaven.

I just tried to read along in the missal and said everything quietly in English. At the Sign of Peace, when everyone turned to their neighbors and shook hands, the large woman in front of me turned around. In Italian, she said softly, *"La pace sia con te."* "Peace," I whispered. I turned to my neighbor and repeated what I remembered: *"La pace."*

When Mass ended, I remained seated in my pew as the others around me stood and left the church. Outside, the church bells rang and parishioners' voices sang out greetings to one another. I was lost within a quiet reflective solitude, thinking about forgiveness. For my Jonathan, and ultimately for myself.

CHAPTER FIFTEEN

Easter was a big deal in Lugano, even if the majority of Swiss residents didn't consider themselves religious. Lugano was still mostly Catholic, more than fifty percent.

Santa Teresa di Lisieux was decked in purple throughout Lent, but on Easter Sunday, the altar was crammed with lilies, hyacinths, daffodils, tulips. White and lavender and yellow and pink everywhere. The bells rang out, not just from Santa Teresa, but also from San Rocco, San Carlo Borromeo, even San Nicolao della Flüe, near the base of Monte Brè. The bells echoed around the lake, from Albogasio to Paradiso.

I dressed up for church, partly out of habit, going back to my childhood, and partly because it felt right to put on my best clothes for Mass, to join with all the other celebrants in the glory of Easter Sunday.

Louie and Francesca were off, and had been since Thursday. Louie informed me on Wednesday that he and his wife were going to Appenzell to visit her family for the Easter weekend. I had been exaggeratedly civil to him ever since the dinner party. I had no solid evidence, other than Donnalee's next-morning admission, which was vague, that anything had transpired between them. She had sent me a thank-you note, in the chubby handwriting of a twelve-year-old, with hearts and smileys to embellish her words: 'Dearest Jennifer, Rodney and I want to thank you for an amazing party!! You are an awesome hostess!!! xoxo, Donnalee' No one else wrote or called to thank me. Not that I was surprised, not that I cared.

And I knew I hadn't heard or seen the last of Donnalee. I figured I could handle it as long as I didn't host another dinner party. Meeting up with her and Rodney at the café would be okay, and probably unavoidable. They were the only friends I had here. I hadn't kept in touch with Michel and Lucia, as I could have. I assumed they were busy with the hotel, but I knew I should at least stop in one day to say hello. It's not that I didn't want friends — I did. Nearly four months in Lugano and I hadn't made enough of an effort, but honestly, the people Donnalee had brought to the party weren't people I was interested in. Lily and Claude were slobs — the bedroom and bathroom they'd helped themselves to looked like a college dorm room after a keg party. Someone had spilled red wine on the sofa and never owned up to it, and they'd all been outraged at having to leave the house so early the next morning. I wished I could talk to Bernie about it, but it felt intrusive to telephone her. I couldn't text her because I still refused to have a cell phone, a decision I found myself regretting more and more frequently. My phone had been a part of me for so long that doing without, purposely, was like being without one of my hands.

I didn't see the large woman in the yellow dress at Mass. I thought I might. The man who sat in front of me had close-cropped hair and blocked my view of the priest at the altar.

The priest spoke in Italian, of course, so I didn't understand any of his homily. I just imagined him speaking about new life, rebirth, beginnings. Was this my new beginning, this time in Lugano? My mind wandered through a mist of memories. Light and shadow crossed paths, merged in sentiments of relief and sadness. Was I grieving enough? Was it okay to be relieved that my husband was gone? I had no answers to my questions.

After Mass ended, I didn't know what to do. My option was to go home or go somewhere else. Perhaps if I had reached out to Lucia, she might have asked me to join them at the hotel for dinner but, while we seemed to be on pleasant terms, I'd given no indication of wanting to pursue a friendship. Bernadette and Gerard might still be in Nice, and all the restaurants were closed for Easter. I walked back to the villa, shrugged out of my dress and shoes. I couldn't just sit around the house all day. I was alone, which was what I'd said I wanted. I couldn't stand it.

I changed into white jeans and loafers and buttoned up a pink shirt. I could ride the boat around the lake, maybe stop in Morcote, where Bernie and I had enjoyed lunch, or I could ride the trains all day. It didn't matter what I did, as long as I stayed in motion. The boats would be crowded today, I reasoned. Tourist season was here. A weekday would be better.

A walk into town might be enjoyable, and the day was sweet with a warm sun and high, puffy clouds, but I called a taxi. Thankfully one arrived within ten minutes.

"Buona Pasqua," the cab driver said as I climbed in.

"Buona Pasqua!" I repeated, hoping he had a family to return to. There was no traffic and we sped through empty streets to the station above the town.

Inside the station it was quiet, except for a couple of families waiting on the platform for a train to arrive. A little girl wearing a frilly white dress and a daisy headband skipped around her parents. Every adult, all seven of them, stared at their phones. No one spoke to anyone.

I walked up to the yellow departures board and saw

that a train to Zurich arrived in nine minutes. That made my decision easier. As I turned back to the ticket window, I almost bumped into someone.

"*Mi scusi*," I said, without raising my head.

"Excuse me, do you speak English?"

I turned my face up to lay eyes on a young man, probably in his early twenties. An enormous backpack balanced on one shoulder. His hair fell into his eyes as soon as he pushed it away, and his boyish face radiated vigor and abundance like a happy child.

"I do. How can I help?"

"Whew! Thank God I picked you. You're American?! I can't speak Italian except for food." He grinned at me as he rolled his eyes and pushed his hair away again. "I wanted to stop here for a couple of nights before I head down to Rome. My friends said I should see the lake. Can you recommend a cheap hotel, by any chance?"

A kid traveling in Europe, in April? He must be a student, I thought. Or a new graduate, exploring the continent.

"You do know nothing is cheap here, don't you?" I smiled.

He lifted the shoulder that didn't hold the backpack. My train would be here any minute. His eyes were bright and filled with hope and his lips seemed to be permanently parted in a good-humored smile.

"Okay, listen. Take the funicular down, then walk toward the lake and find the Hotel Walter. Ask someone for directions if you have to; people here will know the place, it's right on the lake. When you get there, ask for Lucia and tell her that Jennifer sent you. She'll give you a room with breakfast."

"It's not too much?"

I shook my head no. "It'll be okay. I'm Jennifer. Ask for Lucia," I repeated.

He offered me his hand and I took it. "Thanks. Jennifer. Thanks a lot, really. You're awesome." He gave me a wide grin. His mouth was full of big white teeth.

"Go." I watched him lope to the funicular ticket booth and heard my train screech to a halt on the platform behind me. I ignored it. He turned to wave before climbing into the funicular. In another minute the doors closed and the tram began its descent.

I went inside the station and found the tourist information office, staffed by one person.

"Do you speak English?" I asked.

"Of course," the woman said. She had a round, serious face and dark, almond-shaped eyes. Her lavender hijab was dotted with miniature reflective mirrors that seemed to illuminate her with tiny bits of light and rainbow.

"I need to place a local call, but I don't have a cell phone." I turned my palms up.

She offered her phone to me without hesitation.

"Ah, and I don't know the number, either. It's the Hotel Walter."

"Of course," she said again, and pulled the phone back. She consulted a sheet on her desk and punched in the number.

When she handed the phone back to me, it was already ringing. I recognized Lucia's voice.

"*Buona Pasqua*, Lucia! It's Jennifer."

"Oh, Jennifer! *Buona Pasqua*! How are you?" Lucia's voice was light and sunny, like a spring song on a warm breeze.

"I'm fine, thanks. And I owe you a visit soon. But first I need to ask a favor."

"Anything. What can I do for you?"

"A young American man with a big backpack will be coming to the hotel soon. He should arrive within the hour, if not sooner. I don't know his name, but I recommended your hotel to him. I hope you have a room!"

"Oh, that's very kind. We do have one or two rooms available."

"That's lucky! Lucia, he's just a kid. Don't let him pay for anything. I'll pay his bill, okay? I'll be by next week to settle it with you. I think he just needs a couple of nights."

There was silence on the other end of the phone.

"You don't even know him, Jennifer. Why do you do this for a stranger?"

I hadn't understood a word of the priest's homily that morning at Mass, but I recalled the words that the pastor spoke at my husband's service. They were words I would never forget. 'We search for the holy in the midst of the ordinary.'

"Well, we were all young once," I said.

"*Buona Pasqua*." Lucia made a kissing noise into the phone. "We will take care of this traveler."

"*Grazie*, Lucia. See you soon."

I'd missed my train. And suddenly I didn't need to go anywhere.

CHAPTER SIXTEEN

Three days after Easter, another large envelope arrived at the villa. I expected it to contain more mail that Nancy had picked up, but I had just received an envelope from her the previous week, and there were only two sympathy cards in that one. I turned the packet over in my hands. It had been air-expressed and bore a return address in Sausalito, California. A law firm.

Jonathan's ex-wife lived in San Francisco, as far as I knew, and his daughter Deirdre was in Berkeley. I set the envelope on the marble-topped table in the entryway and walked to the kitchen, where I pulled a bottle of San Pellegrino from the refrigerator. Then I picked up the envelope and, with my water, headed outside, where low clouds kept the sun hidden. The air was redolent with hyacinth and peony and the faint odor of wood smoke. The coffee I'd enjoyed two hours earlier rose in my throat as I stared at the envelope. I tried to gather courage to open it. But in my heart I knew it wasn't good.

I scanned the letter, filtering out the legalese as I'd done numerous times over the years, when I read briefs for Jonathan. He'd bring them home for the weekend and ask me to look for language that might be problematic.

169

But today the language was clear. Deirdre was challenging Jonathan's will. He had left her ten thousand dollars and nothing more. She knew he had fifty times that. The house in Providence, the lake house in New Hampshire next to Romney, the cars, the art, the boat we never used that remained docked in Newport, the investment portfolio — all of it had transferred to me upon his death. All but ten thousand dollars. Jonathan knew he was dying, and he'd made certain provisions to give me enough cash until the estate was settled.

I sat as still as a stone. Obviously, Deirdre had learned, or her attorney had, that I was in Switzerland; her lawyer likely had information about the villa and probably knew what I'd paid for the six-month rental. The letter asked for a meeting, and the lawyer, J. Conroy Wickam, wrote that he was available to meet on the East Coast, in Providence or Boston. So they expected me to fly back. Or could my lawyer handle it without me being there? I'd have to call her. I had no intention of involving Jonathan's attorney in this. Considered our family attorney, he and Jonathan went back decades, and I knew he was fond of Virginia. I couldn't trust him to be impartial, not with Jonathan gone.

I had found an attorney four years earlier when I seriously considered leaving my husband. Kathryn Temple was well-known as a divorce lawyer in some higher-profile cases, including Mitch and Bibby

Vickerson's divorce. Mitch was one of the wealthiest real estate developers in the southern New England area, Bibby (Barbara) his devoted wife of thirty-nine years. Kathryn exposed Mitch's ties to organized crime and his addiction to Ritalin. It did not go well for Mitch, but I understood Bibby was living comfortably in Newport.

Kathryn was discreet; the first time we met was on the beach, and as instructed, I wore a caftan, a wide-brimmed straw hat, and oversized, Jackie O sunglasses. She did the same — no one would ever have recognized us. After that initial meeting, we mostly communicated by telephone. In the end, I couldn't go through with it.

"I love him," I confessed to her one morning, three weeks after our initial meeting. "In spite of it all, I still love him."

Her sigh was audible. "Jennifer, from everything you've told me, this man is toxic to you. We can prove he's a cheater. I can get you a lot of money, okay?"

"That isn't it," I said. I knew poverty like an old frenemy. I wasn't afraid to work. Jonathan did more than provide me with financial stability.

"So what is it?" Kathryn asked softly.

"He needs me." And I knew it was true. I could survive without him, but my husband needed me. I also didn't want him involved in a scandal. He'd been foolish a few times, and I'd been able to cover for him. The state would lose a good senator if he resigned in disgrace. Well-liked by his colleagues, brilliant, adored by his constituents. During the time I was in communication with Kathryn, Jonathan had a 72% approval rating — nearly unheard of among the House and Senate. A divorce, especially a contentious one at the hand of man-hater Kathryn Temple, would hurt him politically, emotionally, financially. I wasn't ready to do that to him.

Kathryn wouldn't be the person to contact for this matter. Old Nathan Burns, Jonathan and Virginia's friend, wouldn't help my cause, either. And I was reluctant to bring Nancy into it. She was loyal, and I knew she'd do her best to find someone for me, but I felt it was asking more of her than I should. She was no longer my assistant.

Bernie had told me that she'd been a lawyer — 'a lifetime ago,' she'd said — but maybe she still had connections. I didn't know where else to turn, and that was a problem I'd created by isolating myself from everyone.

I took the letter, folded it back up, and slipped it into its envelope, then went back inside. The house was quiet, as usual. Lifeless. While I certainly didn't want to host another dinner party, full of sodden freeloaders, from time to time I longed for the company of someone. I'd grown weary of having conversations with myself. So I picked up the phone and dialed Bernie's number.

**

"Jen, it's been a very long time since I practiced law, you know that. Decades! I haven't lived in the States for years." Her voice was not unkind, but I heard a tired edge in it.

"I know, I'm just in a bit of a panic here. I don't know anyone well enough to ask." I didn't mention Kathryn, even though I knew Bernie wouldn't pass judgment if I told her I'd considered leaving Jonathan.

"It's been so many years," she said again. I heard her tap her fingernails on the table. "Okay, wait. Can you give me until tomorrow? I'll send out a few feelers."

"Of course. Thanks, Bernie. Truly."

"Jen, you were married to a beloved senator. I'm sure your husband had a lot of lawyer friends who would be happy to help you, you know, as a tribute to him."

How could I explain to her that Jonathan's 'lawyer friends' all preferred his first wife to me? They tolerated me, because they liked him so much. They were polite and mannered and condescending and lecherous. Ask any of them for a favor? No way.

"I'll wait for your call. Thanks again," I said, before letting her go.

Bernie called me later that evening, elated. "I did reach out to my sister Joanie. I hope that was okay. Jen, I never mentioned you, or your husband. I just asked if she could recommend an estate attorney. She doesn't know you're here, and I don't think she would figure it out. I just sent her an email that we have an American client whose *wife* recently passed away, and *he* needs an attorney who specializes in wills. Joanie never asked questions, which is good." Bernie took a breath. "Anyway, can you write this down?" She recited a name, address, telephone number, and email address. I wrote all of it down, and once again I wished I was connected to a computer so I could send the lawyer an email. It would make everything easier. But at least I had a beginning.

As if she could read my mind, Bernie said, "I wish you could send him an email, Jen. Hey, wait! You can! Michael would be happy to set you up at the hotel."

"I don't want to involve him in my personal problems, Bernie. He's busy. I can call the attorney's office tomorrow."

"Well, you could, but you probably know that attorneys rarely take calls from people they don't know.

I mean, you could tell the receptionist who you are…"

"No," I interrupted. "No, I don't want to do that." Better to depend on the kindness of Bernadette's son than on Donnalee or Rodney. Way better. And it was either that or place an overseas call to a law firm and then have to give out all my information before even speaking to the attorney. And lawyers were never sitting by the phone. Lawyers were always in meetings. Plus there was a six-hour time difference.

"So, should I tell Michael to expect you?"

"Sure, thanks. Can I go there tomorrow?" I needed to settle the bill for my young backpacker, too.

"Absolutely. I'll let him know you'll be there mid-morning, okay?" With my spoken affirmation, she added, "Now, when can we get together again?"

I felt tears sting my eyes, I was so grateful she'd asked.

"Soon, please. I don't know what's going to happen with this legal matter. I might have to fly back." My voice broke on that last word. "Sorry, this just really has me rattled."

"Everything will work out, Jen. Have faith. And once you know your schedule, let me know and we'll plan a day."

CHAPTER SEVENTEEN

I drafted a message to the lawyer in Rhode Island, Joseph M. Greeley, Jr., of the firm Greeley Stratton Ellison, and wrote that I had very limited (meaning no) internet access. I requested that he call me directly. He'd add the charges to my bill. I included the information from the Sausalito attorney and, after meeting Michel in the hotel's business office, I scanned the letter and attached it to the email.

"Jennifer, you're free to use our business center anytime," Michel said. "I'm assuming you don't need my help, but I'll be in the adjoining room, so just call to me if you have a question, okay?

"Thanks." I needed a new email address. I was no longer 'FarrahW16' or 'Jenny1806.' I would be 'JLogan6978,' using the postal code for Gandria.

Ten minutes later, Michel poked his head through the doorway and smiled. "Everything good?"

"Fine, thanks. I appreciate being able to use your computer. And it reminds me — yet again — that I should be connected." I sighed. "I really thought unplugging from it all would help, and in some ways, I haven't missed the constant pings from messages and such, but it's nearly impossible to live without internet or a cellphone. I should have realized it." I sent the email, with the letter attached, to Mr. Greeley in Providence.

Michel took a step inside the room and brushed the palm of his hand over the top of his head. "No problem. If you ever want to get one – a phone or a laptop, or both – let me know. I can help."

"Well, I'm only here for another couple of months," I said, the truth of it clinging to my skin.

"You could pick up a pre-loaded phone. You know, pay ahead for it." He shrugged. "Think about it and let me know. And feel free to stop in anytime to check for messages."

"Okay." I'd asked Mr. Greeley to telephone me directly at the villa. A back-and-forth exchange of emails could take us a week to figure anything out.

"So, what's your email address? Just so I have it," Michel asked.

"I'm JLogan6978 at Gmail," I replied.

"Oh! Is that your birthday, then? I was born in 1979," Michel said.

"No, it's the postal code for Gandria. I was born in

1982."

"Ha! I'm older," he said. When he laughed, he looked just like his mother.

I sent the email at ten o'clock in the morning, which meant it was four a.m. in Rhode Island, and unless Joseph M. Greeley, Jr. of Greeley Stratton Ellison worked all night, it would be four to five hours at the earliest before I'd hear back. I stayed for coffee, and settled the bill for the young backpacker, but both Michel and Lucia were too busy to sit around with me, and I made sure not to stay for too long. I thanked them both and said goodbye.

"And let me know if you want to go shopping for technical gadgets!" Michel called after me.

**

Mr. Greeley called at three that afternoon. I'd picked up some sunscreen on the way back to the villa, hoping for a little time by the pool, but instead I paced the marble floor downstairs, expending nervous energy. At noon, I tried to lie down, but couldn't stop fidgeting.

"Mrs. Logan, hello, it's Joe Greeley. Let me first offer my sincerest condolences to you. Senator Logan was a very fine man. I was privileged to meet him twice, once at the retirement party of our founding partner Toby

Stratton, and again when he was keynote speaker for the Bar Association's annual dinner. He is very much missed."

"Thank you," I murmured. It had been four months since Jonathan had died. I had no idea what was going on in Rhode Island, because I didn't keep up with the news. If I was online, would I be reading the *Journal* each morning? "I appreciate it. And thank you for calling me. I assume you've read my message and the letter from Mr. Wickam. Do you think you can help me?"

"Of course, Mrs. Logan. I'd be honored to help you with this matter." He cleared his throat. "From what you've sent me, it appears that Senator Logan's daughter believes she should have received more from his estate. Is...let me see here...is Deirdre Logan Powley his only child?"

"Yes." I'd never asked him, but I was sure that Jonathan would have told me if he had other children. God, please don't let any unplanned children pop up now. "Mr. Greeley, Deirdre didn't like me. Not at all. Her parents had been divorced for years when I met Jonathan, but she harbored tremendous resentment toward me."

"Did the senator's first wife remarry?"

"Virginia? Yes, she remarried." She met a man in

California and married him not long after relocating. Jonathan had told me the story without a trace of envy or bitterness in his voice.

"How old is Deirdre?" Joseph Greeley's voice was soft and gentle, like that of a kind veterinarian with a nervous puppy, I thought. I hoped he was more combative when he needed to be.

"She's thirty-nine," I said. "Five years older than I am."

"Yes, yes. Well. Mrs. Logan, do you want to fly back here? Or would you prefer that I handle all of this alone?"

I hadn't even met Joseph M. Greeley, Jr. If I had a laptop, I suppose I could Google him. But I'd like to at least meet him. And I didn't want Deirdre to think I was afraid to see her. So I allowed my selfish pride to determine my response.

"I guess I should fly back," I said. "I can make arrangements today."

"Just let me know when. I'll take care of everything. If you're able to stay for a week, I'll get Mr. J. Conroy Wickam from Sausalito to come out here." Was there a hint of sarcasm in his voice when he mentioned Wickam's name? I couldn't be sure. I'd have to see Mr.

Greeley's face to know.

**

Bernadette offered to meet me at the airport in Zurich to see me off, but I declined. I was way too nervous about everything to be good company.

"I understand," she said. "I wish I could go with you, Jen, just to keep you company. And visit with my sister, of course," she added with a laugh.

"I wish you could, too. I'll be back next Tuesday morning. God, Bernie, I have absolutely no idea how this is going to go." Did Deirdre have cause? I knew why Jonathan had left her with just a minimal amount. And Deirdre knew, too.

Bernie made a clucking noise into the telephone. "Keep breathing. And trust your attorney. He has your best interests in mind. Remember that." We said goodbye and hung up.

I'd worked with a travel agency in town and had booked a short flight from the Lugano airport to Zurich, then direct from Zurich to Boston. No long scenic train ride this time. And I'd paid an enormous amount of money to fly first-class on short notice, rationalizing that it might be the only time I'd have such luxury ever again. But I was actually able to sleep on the flight, and when the plane touched down in Boston, the sun was slipping under low clouds. It was just after eight in the evening and I had reserved a car and driver to take me to Providence, an hour south of Boston. I spotted an older man holding a card with my name on it and walked up to him.

"You have other luggage, miss?" he asked, offering to take the carry-on bag I held in my hand.

"Nope, just this," I said. A knit dress and pumps for the meeting with the lawyer, and casual clothes for every other day. Everything that I needed was in my one bag.

"Great. Your chariot awaits." I bet he said that to every woman he drove.

Eighty minutes later he pulled up to the Westin Hotel in downtown Providence. The Westin was the newest hotel in the city, and Jonathan had held his last election-night celebration there. I remembered that evening as my driver George pulled the bag from the car's trunk. So many people in the ballroom to congratulate him, even though he'd won re-election by a huge margin.

I tipped George a twenty and confirmed with him my return to Logan Airport the following Monday.

"Hey, your name is Logan. Any connection to the airport?"

"Distant relative to my husband," I said. Would he make the connection?

"Hmm. Logan. You any relation to the senator, the guy who died a few months back?"

"The senator was my husband." I watched as his ears turned bright red.

"Jeez, I'm sorry, miss. I thought maybe he was your dad or something. Jeez. Listen, I'll bring you back," he said, handing me his business card. "Just call or text me the day before to confirm."

I was about to tell him that I didn't text but stopped. I needed a phone. It was so clear, I don't know what I was thinking when I got rid of mine. I didn't want to give in, but I had to face the fact that keeping in touch was a necessity. I could text George for my car. Text Bernie. Text Michel. *Not* text Donnalee. Check my flight status. It was a lovely little experiment, Jennifer unplugged, but time to get real. I had to smile. A year ago, ten years ago, I couldn't imagine getting through one day without my phone.

"You only become as attached to it as you want, you know that," Michel had told me, smiling. "Lucia isn't crazy about hers, either. She forbids the boys to have their phones at dinner. But it's just the way things are."

I knew that. Heck, I'd been the cheerleader for every new upgraded device that was released. There was a Verizon kiosk in the hotel lobby, next to a Starbucks coffee shop.

CHAPTER EIGHTEEN

Deirdre had attended her father's funeral, but we'd only exchanged the briefest of greetings. In the eight years that Jonathan and I were married, I'd been in her company twice, and that included the funeral.

She'd flown out to visit a couple of months after we married, after Jonathan pleaded with her to come. He'd not only persisted, he'd paid for everything. I had asked a lot about his daughter, knowing how much he adored her. I'd asked nothing about Virginia, his ex-wife, and he never spoke of her, even when he told me stories about DiDi, as he called her, as if she were still seven years old.

Virginia and Jonathan had divorced when Deirdre was twelve, a tough time for a girl to be separated from her father (well, any time was bad, wasn't it?). Six months after the divorce papers were signed, Virginia took Deirdre and moved out west, and soon after that she remarried.

When Jonathan proposed to me, I was twenty-six and Deirdre was thirty-one. It was understandable that she was uncomfortable with her father marrying a woman who could have been her younger sister, but I always believed her main concern should have been her father's happiness, and not my age.

When she came to visit, she brought her daughter Skye with her. Newly-divorced and with a toddler, the chip on Deirdre's shoulder was more of a boulder. I was expected to babysit while father and daughter reunited. I didn't mind; Skye was adorable. Deirdre barely spoke to me the entire time — five days — that they stayed in our house. And she made comments like, "Skye, this was my room! It used to be such a pretty yellow, I don't know why anyone would change it to this dull gray," and "Um, do you have any food that a *child* could eat? There doesn't seem to be much here." Jonathan was like clay in her clever, manipulative hands.

Now I sat next to Joe Greeley at a conference table in his office and waited. Greeley had decided we should sit with our backs to the window, facing the door, because it gave us an advantage. Power seats, he'd said, grinning. My lawyer was an affable man of about fifty, I guessed, with short curly hair that was more silver than black. He wore nerdy black glasses that looked anything but nerdy on him, and his ready smile put me at ease immediately. His well-cut, conservative gray suit was offset with a Ninja Turtles necktie.

Deirdre and her attorney were late by ten minutes

and my palms had grown sweaty waiting. They're on California time, I thought. Joe Greeley stood when they entered the room. I did not.

Deirdre gave me a hard look and said, "Hello, Jennifer. You look rested. That villa in Switzerland must be helping you with your grief." As her lawyer made a face and guided her to her chair, Greeley touched my forearm. I knew his gesture was intended to calm me, console me, and keep me from saying a word, but it seemed to have the opposite effect, as Deirdre raised her eyebrows in an exaggerated expression. I looked down at the papers in front of me. Greeley had said I could always pretend to read.

Once everyone was settled, Greeley spoke first. "Thank you for coming east for this meeting. As you know, my client has also traveled a long way. Now, as I understand it, Mr. Wickam, your client believes the amount of money left to her by her late father is…insufficient?"

Wickam fidgeted in his chair, as if his undershorts were causing him considerable discomfort. "It's not what was promised to her. Senator Logan intended for his daughter to be provided for, and he especially intended that there be sufficient funds made available for the education of his only grandchild." He exhaled a feeble, dry cough.

I kept my eyes downcast, even as the typed words in front of me pirouetted and a rumble of nausea heaved deep within my stomach.

Greeley responded. "As you know, the senator's wife is his primary beneficiary. Upon his death, all his property reverts to his spouse, unless otherwise stated in his will."

As Greeley continued to speak, I flashed back to the fight, to the day Deirdre had stormed out of our house, nearly forgetting to take her own daughter with her. I knew she hated me for marrying her father. She hated her father for marrying me.

I raised my eyes to look at Deirdre and was met with such a bitter gaze that I looked down again. I was shaking. She wanted everything. She wanted to leave me with nothing, she had that much contempt for me. Her own marriage had ended badly, before Skye was even born. The man she'd married was a drug addict and had committed armed robbery to feed his habit. He went to prison and had never met Skye.

At our house, Deirdre had been sniping for days, ever since she'd arrived. Little digs that weren't lost on me. Jonathan had ignored most of them. In bed at night, I would complain.

"She's rude. I know she hates me, but there's no

reason for her to disrespect you, too."

He lay next to me, his bare feet playing with mine. He wore expensive cotton pajama bottoms and a worn Yale T-shirt to bed.

"Ssh, sweetheart," he'd crooned in my ear. "She's just getting used to things. For years, when she came to visit me, it was just us. It'll be fine. Now come here." He pulled me on top of him.

The following morning, Deirdre had asked Jonathan if he'd take her to lunch at 'their place,' a fancy steakhouse just outside the city limits. I wasn't invited, of course, and someone had to watch Skye. It was a beautiful spring day, and I decided to take Skye to the little park that overlooked the city. I smiled as they left the house, arm in arm. Daddy's little girl.

Skye and I played in the park — she was afraid of the swings but loved the big plastic elephant. When we returned to the house at two, no one was home, so I put Skye down for a nap and lay down on the sofa in the family room.

An hour later I got up to prepare dinner.

They clattered in around four-thirty, laughing at some inside joke. I was tossing a salad in a big wooden bowl and looked up as they crashed into the kitchen.

"Oh, I can't eat a thing," Deirdre said, laughing. "We had such a huge lunch!" She bumped against her father's shoulder and gave me a sheepish shrug.

"Sorry, sweetheart. We're stuffed." Jonathan winked at me.

I straightened my spine and smiled. "No problem, but I hope you'll sit with me while I eat. I'm actually starving."

"Where's Skye?" Deirdre asked, peering into the family room.

"Oh, she's probably still sleeping," I said. "We had a fun day at the park."

"What time did you put her down?" Deirdre's voice was thick with resentment.

I glanced at my watch. "Around two, I guess."

"What?? You've let her sleep for over two hours? That's just wonderful. Now she'll be up all night." She stormed out of the kitchen and banged up the stairs to where she and Skye shared a room. She slammed a door and I thought, well, that will surely wake the child.

"How would I know that?" I let out a ragged sigh, my appetite gone. "I can't do anything right around your daughter." I vowed not to cry, not there in the kitchen.

Jonathan opened his arms to me. I hated that he was put in the middle of a battle I had no interest in fighting. He shouldn't have to choose between his wife and his daughter, and I was afraid that, if pressed, he'd choose her over me.

Eventually, they came downstairs and sat at the table, at Jonathan's urging. Skye was still groggy but ate bits of cooked chicken and carrots. I picked at my salad and drank chardonnay. Deirdre sulked in her chair, occasionally refilling her wine glass.

Jonathan cleared his throat. "DiDi, I think you owe Jennifer an apology."

"Excuse me? What the hell for?" She stared at him, then me, her eyes flecked with fiery bits of gold.

"Well, she watched Skye today while we went to lunch. She took her to the park. She's babysat every time you and I have gone out, every time we've wanted some time together." I was grateful he didn't say 'adult time' or 'private time,' as he did the other night when we were talking. "Jennifer is my wife now."

"Daddy, please. She's younger than I am. She only married you for your money." Wow, I thought. *In vino veritas?* That was what Deirdre believed.

"That's not true!" I blurted.

It escalated from there. Jonathan and Deirdre shouted at each other. Deirdre resurrected old hurts, Jonathan defended himself. Skye began to wail and Deirdre blamed me for that.

I pushed back from the table as the yelling continued. Picking up my plate, I scraped the remaining lettuce into the trash bin and left the plate on the counter. I hurried upstairs and locked the bathroom door behind me. Even with the door closed, I could still hear them. I ran water in the bathtub until it was nearly full, then stripped off my clothes and stepped in, gasping at the hot water.

The water had cooled by the time Jonathan rapped on the door. "Sweetheart, may I enter?" So formal, my husband.

"Yes."

He tried the knob. "It's locked," he said from the other side.

I hoisted myself from the tub, careful not to splash water on the floor, and opened the drain. I left the towel on the rack and opened the door wide. Jonathan's face broke into a wide grin upon seeing me, water running rivulets down my body.

"You're glistening," he said. "I love you this way." He kicked the door closed and began to unbutton his shirt.

He led me into the big stall shower next to the tub. I was very much aware that Deirdre was within earshot, and it gave me an unreasonable satisfaction. Perhaps my husband felt the same. Either way, she was gone the next morning with barely a goodbye, and Jonathan met with his lawyer the following week.

**

Deirdre didn't have a case, and Greeley proved it. At the end of the meeting, which had eaten up most of the morning, Mr. Wickam grudgingly thanked us for our time.

With Deirdre in the ladies' room, Wickam said, "My client lost the one man who meant everything to her. Naturally, we abide by the law." What did he care, I thought. He'd be paid, and a lot. Two coast-to-coast trips. I figured Virginia would foot the bill. It was a wasted effort for Deirdre. She re-entered the conference room and I could tell that she'd been crying.

"When do you fly back?" I asked, looking at Wickam.

"Tomorrow," Deirdre said, so softly I could barely hear her. She was just a whisper, thin and pale, the fight all drained out of her. Was it about the money? Or something more than that? Was it about claiming herself as her father's first love? "I'll visit Daddy's grave this afternoon."

Jonathan was buried at Swan Point, down near the river in a family plot his maternal great-grandfather had purchased in the late 1800s.

We stood and the attorneys shook hands. Deirdre turned away before I could offer my hand to her, but I don't think she would have accepted it, anyway. Joe Greeley and I stayed behind after they'd left.

"I know she doesn't have a case, Joe," I said, "but ten thousand is a miniscule amount for Jonathan to leave to her. I know he changed his will after they had a big fight years ago. I never knew what he'd done, but I can imagine she's worried about Skye, about providing for her."

"Jen, you're free to do anything you want, you know. Just think about yourself and what you'll need. You're still a young woman."

"Yeah."

"Want to grab lunch? I don't have another meeting until two."

"Thanks, Joe, but no. I've got a few appointments while I'm here. Pretty busy schedule. Listen, thanks for everything."

"Anytime." We shook hands warmly. "Get in touch with me if you need me to handle anything for you."

"I will."

**

I took a taxi to Swan Point. It wasn't far from the house where Jonathan and I had lived, the house now leased to a Brown University professor and his family. I'd have my realtor look into selling it to the university, let them lease it out. I'd never live there again.

Deirdre wasn't at the family plot, so I paid the cab driver and watched him drive away. There was a bench at the edge of the plot, shaded by a big maple, and I sat there in silence. It was so quiet. No one ever spent time in cemeteries anymore. I spotted a person in the distance, a woman walking with exaggerated arm movements. She disappeared as the road dipped down toward the river.

After sitting for about twenty minutes, I stretched and walked in a navigable circle, close enough that I'd see Deirdre if she showed. Perhaps she'd changed her mind. I couldn't relate to the relationship she had with Jonathan; I had never had a relationship with my father. I didn't even know who he was, and never bothered to find out. The only thing my mother ever told me about him was that he was tall and blond, and had a poster of Farrah Fawcett on his wall. "He loved her," she'd said. "Lot more'n me, that's for damn sure."

Deirdre did have a father, though. Jonathan didn't run for the senate until after he'd divorced Virginia, but while he was married he was a successful lawyer. He was there to bring DiDi to grade-school father-daughter dances, to play Santa, to hoist her on his shoulders at a parade, to teach her to swim. And then he was gone. Of course she missed him. Of course she was angry. She'd been let down by her father and by her husband.

I was seated on the bench, staring at my hands, when I heard the car pull up. I stayed still until I heard the car door open and shut, then I stood and turned to face Deirdre.

"I really just wanted to spend a little time alone with him," she said.

"I understand, and I'll leave you in a minute. But I need to say something."

She shifted her weight, and hid her hands behind her back. Her eyes darted about.

"Listen." I bent my head and concentrated on using words that wouldn't set her off. "I'm sorry it came to this. It wasn't my intention." So far it was lame on my part, but Deirdre stood silent.

"I don't want you to worry…"

"What does that mean, Jennifer?"

I took a deep breath. "I don't believe your father would ever deny Skye anything. I'd like to ask my attorney to sct up a trust fund for her education." I didn't know Deirdre well, but if she was simply after cash, I'd know by her reaction. A trust fund was just that — money set aside for the future, for Skye.

"You're willing to do that?"

"Yes," I said. "If you agree, I'll put it into motion before I leave." I waited and watched her. She seemed intent on maintaining no expression, but her mouth twisted in pain before she let out a anguished sob. Her shoulders shook and she brought her fist to her mouth, as if it could stop her from crying.

"I hated the way things ended between us," she choked. "I had so many chances to say I was sorry, and I didn't." She dissolved into her grief and I went to her without thinking. I wrapped my arms around her, and she didn't pull away. "I'm sorry, I'm sorry," she kept repeating.

"Shush now, it's okay." I stroked her hair and spoke

in soft, low tones as if I were consoling a distraught child. "Come sit for a minute." We moved to the bench, where Deirdre gulped air and swiped at her tears.

"I'm a failure," she said, her voice broken and rough.

"No, no, don't say that. Look at your beautiful daughter. How old is she now?"

"Almost eleven. I can't believe it." Deirdre's youth was gone, her face was tired.

"I did love your dad, you know. He was smart, and witty, and cared so much about people, regular, everyday people. He was very much loved."

"Did he make you happy?" she wiped away the last of her tears.

"Of course," I replied without thinking. And quickly added, "And I did everything I could to make him happy, too."

"I know," she said, smiling at me for what was very possibly the first time ever. "I know you did."

CHAPTER NINETEEN

The following day I bought a phone. I was surprised at how expensive it was — eight years earlier, I'd gotten my phone for free by signing up for a plan. And the phones I'd had during my marriage were always bought by someone else. I never worried about the cost. A couple of months after we married, Jonathan brought home a new phone for me and said it was fancier than the one I had. That much was true. He was technically savvy, more so than most people his age. I realized later that he used the phone to hide calls and messages from me. He asked me not to call his office in Washington. I didn't need to speak to his secretary or one of his aides. I'd call or text him on his phone and he'd get back to me when he wanted.

The salesperson might have marked me as an easy upsell, I don't know. He started talking to me as if I was buying my first cellphone. I raised my hand to stop him. "As long as I can use it overseas," I said. "Just set me up. Please."

"Not all cellphones work in every country," he said.

"I'm returning to Switzerland. If I travel at all, it will

be to France or Italy. Can you do what needs to be done so I can use the phone there?"

"Yeah, yeah. You want a quad-band phone. It'll take a few minutes, but I can get you set up."

"Great. Whatever you need to do."

An hour and many dollars later, I was back in my hotel room and composing an email to Michel and Bernadette. 'I am now reconnected!' I typed. 'Here's my number. I'm flying back Monday night. Everything is fine. If you need me to pick anything up for you while I'm here, text me! See you soon. Jen'

I still had the rest of the day to myself. I would visit my mother on Sunday, even though I knew she probably wouldn't recognize me. Obligation, I thought to myself. Obligations die hard. She was in the best facility and I knew she was cared for, but my presence there might be a simple reminder to the staff that she wasn't completely forgotten.

And I thought about contacting Robbie. My flight wasn't until Monday evening. It would be very short notice, but maybe he'd meet me for lunch before I had to get to the airport. Nothing complicated, but a chance for us to close the chapter of our lives that wasn't terribly well written. I assumed he was still in Boston.

I opened my phone and searched for him online, and discovered that he had an exhibition at a gallery on Newbury Street. Wow, his first real show that I knew of. I was happy for him. I could take the train to Boston in the late morning on Monday, maybe catch up with Robbie before flying out. All my ends would be tied up. I called the gallery. A breathy, high-pitched voice answered. "Good morning. Nuovo."

"Hello, yes, I'm calling about your current exhibition. Robbie, I mean Robert Trudell?"

"Yes, he is here." She had a ghost of a lisp and an accent I couldn't place.

"Great. And, uh, is the artist on the premises? I mean, is it possible to meet him?"

She paused. "Are you looking to buy?"

"Perhaps, yes. Probably." I never really cared much for Robbie's work, if I was being truthful. His paintings were dark and brooding. I suppose it was that they were reflective of the frustration and anger he felt. But maybe I should help him out, I thought, and buy one of his pieces. "I'd like to stop in on Monday, late morning."

Her voice was like wispy clouds that skittered across the sky. "Mr. Trudell usually paints in the morning." Really, I thought. He used to prefer nights. "I can let him know that you will be here, Ms.?"

Now it was my turn to pause. "Lucia," I said without thinking. "Just Lucia is fine. Thank you." And I ended the call before she could say anything more.

What was wrong with me? Either I wanted to see him or I didn't. I wasn't someone who played games. If I went to the gallery, I would go as Jennifer Logan and see Robbie.

**

On Sunday morning, I went to church, but it wasn't the same as going to Santa Teresa di Lisieux. I missed the Italian that I couldn't understand. Funny, I'd say the prayers softly in English, and I usually daydreamed through the sermon. In St. Bartholomew's on the east side of Providence, I listened to the homily and zoned out during the rest.

As Mass ended, I joined the group exiting the church and stepped into brilliant sunshine. My heart was light and I looked forward to a walk along familiar streets.

"Mrs. Logan?" An unfamiliar voice behind me caught my attention. What made me think I wouldn't be recognized in Providence, where I'd lived in the public eye for eight years?

"Hello," I said to a man who looked vaguely

familiar. He was about my age, I guessed, had thick brown hair and perfectly-manscaped eyebrows. He strode up to me with his right hand outstretched.

"It's Trevor Dawson from Channel 12," he said, as my throat closed. Wasn't he the investigative reporter who always did pieces on corruption within government? "How are you doing, Mrs. Logan?"

I stopped briefly to address him. "I'm doing all right, thank you for asking," I said. I hadn't taken his hand, and he put it in his pocket. I kept walking away from the church.

"Are you still in Providence?" he asked, falling into step next to me, too close, his left arm brushing against my right as I walked. I stopped again and pulled sunglasses out of my purse.

"I am today." He couldn't read anything on my face except the tight thin line of my lips.

"That's cryptic!" He grinned, and I remembered his uneven, unnaturally white teeth. He should have fixed those teeth before going into television. It had always unnerved me when I'd see him on the news.

"It was good to see you," I said, knowing he saw right through my lie. But I assumed people lied to Trevor Dawson all the time. He was used to it. I began walking faster, grateful for my comfortable shoes.

"Mrs. Logan?" I stopped once more. This would be the last time. I didn't need to be polite to the press anymore. "Would you be available for an interview? Something about the senator's legacy?"

"Of course not, Trevor. I am most definitely *not* available. But you have a nice day." And I gave him my brightest smile, all perfectly straight teeth.

**

My mother was dressed in a yellow velour track suit and white sneakers. Her hair was gray and lank, and the nurse on duty explained that their regular hairdresser had just had a baby and they were hoping to get a replacement soon. "This week or next, for sure," she said. Otherwise, my mother was clean and groomed. Her wheelchair was set and locked in front of the nurses' station, along with two others. The other two occupants were sleeping, but my mom watched me as I arrived, and never took her eyes off me as I approached her.

"Hi, Mom. It's good to see you," I said, bending at the waist to kiss her pallid cheek. She giggled like a schoolgirl and pretended to swat me away. "Did you have breakfast today?"

There was no response and her eyes had gone vacant.

The nurse responded. "She did. Kathleen, you ate scrambled eggs and toast, didn't you? And you really liked them!"

I took a couple of steps to the wide desk that served as the nurses' station. "I'm sorry, I don't know your name," I said.

"I'm June. I don't think we've met, Mrs. Logan, but I'd know you anywhere. And I loved your husband. I cried so hard when he died." She held my hand in both of hers and looked to be on the verge of tears again. Her bosom heaved under a cotton top patterned with pink and purple cats.

"Thank you. And how is Kathleen doing? Is there anything I should know?"

June tapped a short unlacquered fingernail against her cheek. "Well, she continues to decline, as I'm sure you know. Let me grab her chart." She pulled eyeglasses off the top of her head and slid them on, then turned back to rifle through binders set up along the back wall. "Yes, the doctor visited her last week and noted decreased cognitive function. She eats breakfast in the morning, almost always, but doesn't have much interest in food after that. And she's alert now, which is good, but she'll sleep a lot in the afternoon."

"Any more episodes?"

"We keep her medicated, Mrs. Logan. She's pretty calm, as you can see."

I glanced over to my mother, who was nodding off in her chair. A strap across her sunken chest kept her from falling forward. The woman who was drunk during most of my childhood and adolescence was a stranger to me. She had cirrhosis of the liver, had had multiple strokes, had lost her ability to speak, had no use of her right side, was incontinent, and was prone to seizures. She was fifty-eight years old.

"I'm going to take her to the solarium," I said, unlocking her wheels and pushing her toward the open, sunny room that was at the end of the corridor.

"Nice to see you, Mrs. Logan," June chirped.

I sat with my mother for an hour and a half. She slept. I watched the Food Network on television. No one came into the room. At twelve-thirty, I wheeled her to the dining room and relinquished her to an aide, who smiled into my mother's face.

"Kathleen, are you hungry? We have baked fish and mashed potatoes today!"

The food on her plate was pureed and white, except for a small orange mound of butternut squash. The aide secured a cotton bib around my mother's neck and crooned words of encouragement to her as she attempted to put small spoonsful of food into her mouth. It was time for me to leave.

VILLA DEL SOL

CHAPTER TWENTY

On Monday, before I checked out of my room at the hotel, I called Joe Greeley on his cell phone. It went directly to voice mail. Maybe he didn't answer if he didn't recognize the number. I left him a brief message and reiterated my desire to set up a trust fund for Skye. Then I added half of that amount for Deirdre's immediate access. She'd be surprised and, I hoped, pleased. There was plenty of money for everyone. I gave Greeley the number for my realtor and indicated my desire to sell the Providence house and the boat, and I instructed him to transfer ownership of the New Hampshire lake house to Deirdre. She could keep it or sell it. I retained the investment portfolio.

I picked up my carry-on bag, descended in the elevator, settled my bill at the front desk, and waited for a cab. I had cancelled the car the previous evening in a text. George would understand.

It took less than five minutes to get to the Providence train station, and I bought a one-way ticket to Boston. We pulled into South Station just after ten. Being back in Boston felt like stepping into an old pair of loafers. Easy and comfortable. I knew the area well.

211

After securing my carry-on in a locker at the train station, I bought a cup of coffee. People wandered around the station, not in the frenetic rush of early morning. Nearly every person toted a cardboard cup in one hand and a cell phone in the other. The big schedule board above my head clicked over and I involuntarily looked up. A voice over the public-address system announced the arrival of a train to Portland on track two. Another train to New York City on track one.

I had ten hours to fill before my flight. Even if I arrived at the airport two hours ahead of time, that left me with eight hours, and I couldn't spend eight hours in the gallery. Maybe Robbie and I could have a leisurely lunch that took me to three. We did have a lot to talk about, and I was excited to hear about his career. I used the ladies' room to check my hair and makeup.

It was my chance for closure. It would likely be the last time I'd ever see him. How lucky to know when that last time is? How lucky to be able to say all the things that should be said — to be forgiving and kind and compassionate. To say goodbye with love.

Why was I so nervous? It was nearly nine years since we'd broken up. We were kids then, full of idealism and promise. I loved the idea of Robbie as a starving artist, of me as a restaurant hostess, of us living in an old loft above an abandoned match factory that had a leaky faucet and a noisy radiator. Eating ramen noodles, making love whenever the mood was there, and it was there so often. It all worked well for a year or so, but then our electricity was shut off and I was stealing toilet paper from the restaurant supply closet. I could barely support myself, and then I had to support him, too.

When I'd suggested he look for something part-time, he gave me a blank stare.

"A few hours a day, babe. Anything would help at this point. Home Depot is hiring in the paint department."

"You're kidding. The paint department? Because I paint?" He tossed a rag onto the floor. Paint splatters were everywhere.

"Well, maybe I could get you in at the restaurant. The waiters there make great money at night."

He altered his stance, like he was in a bullring and I'd just waved a red cloth. "You cannot be serious," he said. "Not only do I have zero experience waiting tables, when am I supposed to paint?" He sat on his wooden chair and it creaked. I imagined it breaking and Robbie falling on the floor and I almost laughed.

"You probably wouldn't have to start until three or four in the afternoon."

He stood up, but continued to glare at me. "Jesus, Jen. I thought you believed in me."

"I do!" Then, more quietly, "I do. I'm not saying you stop creating art. But we need money to live. You need to see a dentist for that tooth, our furniture is falling apart, and our car is going to die any day now."

He shook his head slowly, like our dire situation was incomprehensible to him. Our rent had just gone up a hundred bucks a month, because landlords were realizing that a lot of rich folks would buy lofts like ours, sink money into them, and turn them into cool city living spaces. We lived month-to-month, and I was afraid we'd be given notice to vacate.

I was fortunate that I could get a decent meal at the restaurant. I tried to bring some food home to Robbie after my shift, but if he was painting, he just brushed me away.

At the end of May, one of the waitresses said her roommate was going abroad for the summer. I asked if I could live with her. Kate rented a condo on Beacon Street, a breezy two-bedroom with a balcony. My moving in for the summer would help everyone — the roommate would have her share of the rent covered (she even reduced my share by fifty a month to show her gratitude), Kate was happy enough to have me live there, and I'd have a secure place to live for the summer, at less than I was currently paying for the loft, since I was shouldering the entire rent. I was elated, until I had to break the news to Robbie.

His voice stayed calm, which was in some ways scarier than if he'd exploded in rage. He was washing his brushes in the kitchen sink. The canvas he was working on was an abstract of brown and gray and an ugly shade of green. I had no idea what it represented. Maybe us.

"When are you moving out?" he asked, as he jammed the brushes in an old mayonnaise jar.

"Rob, let's talk about this, honey."

"What's to talk about? You've made your decision. Time to move on."

"Yeah. Listen, Robbie, I need to feel secure, okay? You know?" He didn't answer me. He had no interest in talking.

"I'm going out for a while," he muttered. He grabbed his key and left. When I woke in the morning, he was still gone. I could have called his friends, but I didn't. I packed up two bags and brought them with me to work. Robbie and I never said goodbye.

I had considered leaving him a note, had actually sat at our rickety table and held my pen above the paper, trying to find the right words. There were no right words. I had to leave. I had to take care of myself.

Three weeks later, Jonathan Logan walked into the restaurant.

**

I arrived at the gallery shortly before eleven. It was a quiet Monday. When I opened the front door, tiny bells tinkled to announce my arrival.

I paused and took in my surroundings. Robbie had discovered color. His paintings filled the space with vibrancy – yellows and greens, blues and purples, pink and red and turquoise.

A young woman emerged from a back room. She looked like an African princess, regal in her stature, the curve of her cheek, the black hair cropped close to her beautifully-shaped head. Silver earrings dangled against her neck, nearly touching her collarbone. Her eyes were large and round and nearly black. She was stunning.

"Good morning!" she said in the same breathy, high-pitched voice I'd heard on the telephone. I tried to place the accent. Jamaican? "May I show you anything in particular? Or are you here simply to see the beautiful art?" Her lips, full and painted dark red, curved upwards as her eyes roamed the gallery. Every time she moved, the earrings bounced and glittered against her skin. I lifted my hand to my earlobe without thinking, to the plain gold stud that lay in my lobe.

"Is the artist here? These are quite marvelous," I said, meaning it. I had to tell Robbie what beautiful works he'd created.

She narrowed her eyes at me. "Are you Lucia? The one who called?"

Lucia. Oh yes. Now what would I do when this woman introduced me to Robbie as Lucia?

"Um..."

"I'm so sorry, Lucia," she said. "But Robert is not here. He will be perhaps here late in the afternoon." She called him Ro-Bear, like the French would do. "Do you know Ro-Bear?"

"I did, a long time ago. Actually, my name is not Lucia. We must have had a misunderstanding on the phone. My name is Jennifer." I smiled, hoping the 'misunderstanding' would be forgotten. She cocked her head, and her long neck twisted like a swan's.

"Ah, you are Jennifer. Yes, Jennifer. Ro-Bear has spoken of you." She stood a head taller than me, and I was inexplicably intimidated by her presence. I couldn't say why.

But my heart lifted at her words. "He has spoken of me?! Really?" Maybe he wasn't angry with me anymore. After all, he did come to Jonathan's funeral, and he'd contacted Nancy. Maybe he wanted to talk, too.

"I am Charmaine, his wife. He said that you two were together many years ago. And you are married now as well, yes? It's very nice to meet you." She offered a slender brown hand. Thin gold bangles, three of them, jangled on her slim wrist.

It was as if a freight train was speeding through the gallery. I couldn't hear any of the words she spoke after 'wife,' even as I watched her full lips move and smile and laugh. I took a few steps back and bumped into a pole that was in the middle of the gallery. I leaned against it for support and took several deep breaths.

"Would you like some water, Jennifer? Perhaps tea? While you look around? I'm so sorry Ro-Bear is not here to say hello to you." She left me as she disappeared in the back, presumably to get me some water or tea. Or both.

Of course he was married. Why wouldn't he be? Did I really think he'd pine for me all these years? Did I think he came to the funeral to capture me, the grieving widow? I was a fool. And I wanted to run out of the gallery but my feet wouldn't move.

My eye caught a painting on the far wall, as far away from Charmaine as possible. I floated toward it. It was our match factory building at night, lit up with fluorescence. Our dark street was dotted with headlights. It was different than all the other paintings.

"Ah, yes, that one," she said behind me. I normally would have been startled, but her voice was so soft and light, it was as if she was an angel on my shoulder, whispering soothing prayers into my ear. "Ro-Bear said you both lived in this building."

I nodded, at a loss for words. "Would he sell it to me?" I couldn't turn around, couldn't let her see what this painting had done to me.

"Of course, Jennifer. I think Ro-Bear would sell it only to you."

**

I checked for messages as I sat in the Isabella Gardner Stewart Museum's cafeteria. One was from Michel: 'Great, Jennifer! I promise not to send lots of texts. Safe travels back.' And the second was from Bernie: 'Thank you, Jen. Do you arrive ZRH tomw morning?'

I didn't need to respond to Michel. I opened Bernie's message and typed out a reply. 'Yes but have flight to

LUG. Arr LUG 1pm' I hit send and set the phone down.

I sipped tea and nibbled on quiche and, like everyone else, stared at my phone, waiting for a response.

Within a minute, there it was. 'Great. Will meet you at LUG airport. Hope all is well.'

I wanted to tell her everything, but it would have to wait. I typed 'OK.'

I tucked my phone back in my purse and checked my watch for the umpteenth time. I had purchased a very large painting, a Robert Trudell original, and I had nowhere to put it. I couldn't ship it to the villa, I'd only be there for a couple more months. I couldn't ship it to the Hotel Walter — what would they want with it? Their art was of the Alps and edelweiss and beautiful vistas. I couldn't send it to the nursing home — they wouldn't want it, either. So I asked Charmaine if it could be kept at the gallery for the time being. She was gracious and kind and said of course they would keep it on display.

I paid for the painting and watched as she affixed a small card on the wall next to it that read 'SOLD.' I assumed that she would probably have called Robbie as soon as I'd left. Maybe she texted him. I wondered why Robbie had come alone to Jonathan's funeral, why Charmaine did not know that I'd lost my husband. I wondered if Charmaine knew that Robbie had contacted me. According to the note I'd received from Nancy a few months back, he'd called looking for me. And now I had gone looking for him. Of course, I didn't know he was married. If I had known, I don't know if I would have even gone to the gallery.

I didn't want a relationship with him, even more so knowing that he had a wife. Just as I despised my husband's adultery, so I despised it in others and wouldn't be a party to it. Besides, the past was past. I'd been hoping to mend that fence with Robbie, and maybe by purchasing the match factory painting, I had. But there would be no more contact from me to him. Even the painting, they could keep it. It belonged in the gallery, not on a wall in any home I would live in.

Perhaps it was the high I felt from reconciling with Deirdre that had spurred me on. I had a lot of regret about the way things had ended between Rob and me, and I was genuinely happy for his success. He'd done it. As I was leaving the gallery, I said to Charmaine, "Please tell Rob that I wish him continued success. He has great talent."

Charmaine hugged me, and I could feel the bones in her spine through her thin cotton shirt. "Oh, Jennifer, thank you, thank you. I will tell Ro-Bear."

I opened the door, listened to the little bells, and

stepped out into the sun and out of Robbie's life forever.

CHAPTER TWENTY-ONE

The flight back to Switzerland was, in a word, luxurious. First-class tickets were terribly expensive, that was true. I wouldn't make a habit of it, even though I could afford it. It was obscene, actually, but I tried to rationalize the expense in my mind. Just this time. This was different. I'm not losing everything. I've given nearly half of Jonathan's fortune to Deirdre and Skye, and I still have enough. More than enough.

I slept for nearly the entire flight, blanketed with worry-free dreams.

The airplane touched down right on time, so Swiss. I cleared Customs easily. The officer glanced at my passport stamp, but asked no questions, and stamped me back in. I picked up my carry-on bag and made my way to the gate where my little plane waited to take me to Lugano.

True to her word, Bernie was waiting for me in the airport lounge. She held up her hand in greeting but I thought she would be happier to see me.

"Hi!" I said, embracing her. "So nice of you to meet me. It wasn't necessary."

"Well, yes, it was. It is," she said. Before I could ask her what she meant, she pointed. "Is that your only bag?"

"Yes. What's going on?" It was a déjà-vu experience, like when she met me at the Zurich airport and told me the villa wasn't ready. I sensed something awful about to happen.

"I received some news the other day," Bernie said, tugging at one of her ringlets. "The owner of the villa has sold it."

"Sold it?! What?!" I stopped walking.

"It's okay, Jen. It'll be okay. Apparently, he's been having financial difficulties and his loan went into default."

"Oh, my God." I sat down on a nearby bench and searched her face. "Do I have to leave?"

"No," she said firmly. "You have a contract until the middle of July. Wait. No, until the end of July because of the delay. You're there until the end of July, okay? I've been in contact with the new owner."

"And he – she? – understands?"

Bernie looked away. "If I'm being honest, he understands. He's not thrilled about it. He toured the house while you were away, and made an offer to the bank that was accepted, because of the default situation."

"I was only gone a week! Wait, he was inside?"

She shrugged. "Jen, there was nothing you could have done. Even if you were here, you would have had to let him in. The bank was eager to move the property. He made the offer. A *cash* offer," she added with a meaningful look.

I could estimate what he'd paid. A property like that went for millions, even if it was a bank sale. I could never have bought it outright, anyway. "Whatever. So, you've met him?"

"No, I've just spoken with him on the phone. He's British, so at least we didn't have a language issue. He's...brusque."

"Brusque, great. Oh, Bernie."

"I know, sweetie. I'm sorry."

"It's not your fault," I said, exhaling. "Okay, let's go."

∗∗

The house felt different. I'd begun to think of it less as a rental and more like home. Until I heard the news. Bernie drove up the gravel drive that curved behind the house and set the parking brake. We entered through the back door and stepped into the kitchen.

It was spotless, of course. A note from Francesca was stuck to the door on the inside:

Ben tornata, Jennifer. Food inside refrigerator.

I opened the fridge door and retrieved an oval bowl of pasta salad, with chunks of artichokes, olives, chicken, tomatoes. There was another bowl full of fruit – melon and berries and pineapple. A small round loaf of dark bread sat on a wooden board, half-wrapped in a white linen cloth, with a serrated knife by its side.

"Might as well eat," I said. We brought the food outside to eat by the pool that sparkled aquamarine diamonds in the midday sun.

"Ciao!" Louie called from the terrace above us. We turned and I raised my hand in greeting.

"I hope he doesn't come down," I whispered. "I'm still mad at him from the party." With Bernie's questioning look, I explained what I believed to have happened. She sighed.

"You don't know for sure, though."

"No, but I bet it happened. That Donnalee. And him! With his wife next door." I jabbed at a piece a chicken.

"Try not to think about it. Focus on yourself." Bernie looked pretty. Under the big yellow umbrella, her hair took on a sunlit tone.

"I have three bathing suits, if you feel like swimming later. I feel as though I haven't used the pool enough. And the days are speeding by now."

Bernie smiled at me. "Jen, again, I'm so sorry about all this. You're taking it well." She raised her eyebrows, waiting for my reaction.

I shrugged. "What can I do? I don't own the place. I couldn't have bought it, even if I had known about the sale. I was back in the States, dealing with my own problems. I just don't want this guy hassling me for the time I have left here." Neither of us had touched the bread. We both were trying to avoid it, I knew. But it sat there, taunting me, knowing my weakness, and before I knew what my hands were doing, I'd sliced through it. "Do you want the end piece?" I held it in my hand, offering the best part of the bread to my friend. She shook her head and copper curls danced around her face.

"Well, he'd better not bother you. And if he does, I want to know right away. Text me," she added, bumping my arm.

After my laugh, Bernie leaned forward, her eyes serious. "So, tell me. How did everything go?"

"Oh, Bernie. Well, Joe Greeley is a doll. I'm glad he's my lawyer. Deirdre, poor Deirdre." I told her about the fight that had happened so long ago, and about meeting her in the cemetery. "She was so sad, so bitter. I think it was her guilt that had made her hard. She missed her dad."

"Of course. I still miss my dad. And my mom."

I didn't respond. She laid her hand on mine. "How is your mother?"

"Failing." I gave her a short synopsis of my mother's health, but it was all so complicated, and I didn't want to go there. I turned the subject back to Deirdre. "I took care of her. Jonathan had changed his will to punish her, which was wrong. She and her daughter will be alright."

"I'm really happy to hear this, Jen."

"Yeah, me, too. I hated the divide between us. We both lost him." I picked at the remainder of my pasta salad, not hungry anymore.

"You miss him, I know."

I didn't respond. I couldn't, really. As close as I felt to Bernadette, I wasn't yet able to share with her my deepest regrets and doubts about my marriage.

"I loved him," I said, looking up. "Our marriage

wasn't perfect."

"No marriage is perfect, you know that."

"What about you and Gary?"

She smiled. "It was about as close to perfect as it could get with Gary," she admitted. "Too short a time for us. I guess I was referring to Gerard. We spend a lot of time apart. He loves being outside. I don't. In our free time, we do separate things."

"Would you rather go inside now?" I asked.

"No! No, it's lovely out here. Look, I enjoy a nice walk, a boat ride on the lake. Gerard is different. He runs, he climbs mountains, he rappels back down. He does all these things without me because I have no interest in them." She shrugged, a dismissal of the way things were. She inspected her fingernails before meeting my eyes. She was near tears and instinctively, I reached out. She shook her head. "When he's home, it's as if he's still away. I'm alone in my marriage. And I'm just waiting for him to tell me he wants a divorce. Maybe he's already met someone, someone who wants to climb mountains with him." She gave a short, hard laugh. "It wouldn't surprise me, Jen. We haven't been intimate in nearly a year."

I was shocked, but tried not to show it. I thought of

Bernadette and Gerard as the couple on the cake, both confident in their skins, free to pursue their interests, even if they didn't always mesh. I hadn't realized Bernie was so lonely.

"Do you still want to be married to him?"

She used both hands to pull her hair back from her face. Her forehead was smooth and unlined. For a woman of nearly sixty, with such fair skin, she was luminous, and easily looked twenty years younger. Just a reminder to keep using sunscreen, I told myself, as I scooted under the umbrella and out of the hot, punishing sun.

"I don't know. I was on my own for a while after Gary died. I suppose if Gerard and I split, I'd move down here, be closer to Michael and Lucia and the kids. I wouldn't mind, I guess." She looked up and smiled again. "Just saying it out loud forces me to face what could happen."

**

I returned to church on Sunday. During Mass, I tried to say the words out loud, reading from the little book in the pew. Since I knew the prayers, the words made more sense to me. But I was still unable to follow the homily. But that morning, I didn't daydream about Francesca's food, or the sparkling pool, or anyone sitting in front of me. Instead, I thought about Jonathan. Silently, I forgave him for his infidelities, the few I knew about and the others I didn't. I forgave him his impatience, his anger, his distance with me. I had absolved him before he died. He had asked me to forgive him as he clutched my hand, his face ashen, his red-rimmed eyes frantic. He begged me for forgiveness. Whether it was for everything in the past, or for what he was about to do, I couldn't be sure. But I said yes.

I had asked him if he wanted a minister, or a spiritual adviser, and he said no. His doctor and his trusted friend lingered outside our bedroom. They wouldn't enter until I had left. I wasn't yet ready to leave, though.

"Are you in pain?" I asked.

He squeezed my hand. "Yes, my love. Very much." I reached for the morphine. I knew how to administer the pre-filled dose.

He stopped me. "No, no more," he said.

"It will help."

He shook his head no. "I don't want to be a burden to you."

"You're not, my love."

"Yes," he croaked.

I stroked his cheek. "It goes with the vow. In sickness and in health," I said.

"Until death parts us," he whispered. "Go get some sleep."

I kissed him on the forehead and left the bedroom, and just as I had drifted into a light doze, Dr. Mitchell shook me awake and told me that my husband was dead.

Mass had ended and I hadn't realized it until people around me stood and filed out of their pews.

"Dear Lord, please forgive him," I whispered.

CHAPTER TWENTY-TWO

The new owner of the villa showed up on Tuesday. I had gone out for my regular morning walk on the Olive Trail and was thinking about a swim. My pool days were numbered, I knew, and I made a promise to myself that I would try to fill each of the remaining days with something good.

As I walked back up the gravel driveway to the rear of the house, I spied a black sports car parked up under the tree. The car was low to the ground and shiny — an Alfa Romeo? Maserati? At first I thought someone must be visiting Louie and Francesca, but before I could unlock the back door, a voice called out.

"Pardon me? Hello?"

A British accent. Ah, the owner. He emerged from the shiny car, tall and dressed in black on a warm summery day. Mirrored sunglasses hid his eyes. He looked more Italian than British, except for his fair skin and golden hair. Then he spoke again.

"Ms. Logan? I'm Nicholas Radcliffe." He took long strides toward me with his right hand extended. The other hand was behind his back.

I shook his hand, but kept my own sunglasses on. He could remove his first, I thought. We were both armored, and hiding. Bernie had said he was 'brusque.' I looked at his mouth. Full lips that did not smile at me. Reddish-gold stubble, carefully maintained. Something told me this man liked mirrors.

"You're the new owner of this villa." I stated it as fact.

"Yes. So you've been informed."

"I have. And I'm sure you've been informed that my contract to live here extends until the end of July." I put my hands on my hips, then removed them and clasped them behind my back. I was sure Louie and Francesca were listening to our exchange, probably from their terrace behind the big tree. They were camouflaged.

"Could we go inside to talk?" he said.

I didn't want to invite him inside. Did I have to? What would he do if I refused? It didn't seem worth it to find out.

I made a show of exhaling before unlocking the back door. He held it open as I entered the kitchen. My swim and my lunch would have to wait, and, as if on cue, my stomach rumbled loudly.

Nicholas smiled as I felt my cheeks burn. "Francesca

mentioned there's food," he said. "I'm hungry, too. Why don't we have something to eat." Without waiting for an answer, he opened the refrigerator and pulled out a platter. I felt like a guest in the villa. My villa. His villa. The antipasto looked delicious. He set a bottle of wine on the counter. So that's what he was hiding behind his back.

"Will you join me in a glass of wine?" he asked.

"No, thank you. Water's fine." He will not rattle me, I vowed silently.

He shrugged. "Corkscrew?" I opened a drawer and handed it to him. While he opened the wine, I took a bottle of San Pellegrino from the refrigerator and poured a glass for myself, adding a slice of lemon. Nicholas carried the platter to the table, which was set for two. Dammit, Francesca!

"Oh, the baguette," he said, sprinting back into the kitchen and returning with the long loaf of bread and a serrated knife.

There was a glass vase on the table, filled with fresh flowers — daisies in pink and orange and yellow. I had not put flowers on the table. My cook had turned into a matchmaker and I was not happy about it.

"May I?" he inquired, and used a giant spoon to serve

tortellini, mozzarella balls, and vegetables onto my plate. I held up my hand.

"That's plenty," I snapped, regretting the sharpness in my voice. I would be polite. I would not allow him to see how difficult this was for me. "Thanks."

He was languid in his actions, slow to pour pale yellow wine into his glass, slow to fill his plate. He unfolded a cheery coral-colored linen napkin and placed it in his lap.

He had removed his mirrored sunglasses. Nicholas Radcliffe had greenish-gray eyes and pale eyelashes and brows to match his reddish-blond hair. His hair was thick and shaggy. He wasn't the kind of guy I'd go for, but he wasn't bad-looking.

"You sure you don't want a glass of wine? I brought it especially for our first meeting." I couldn't tell if he was joking. Did he think I'd be in a celebratory mood?

"I'm fine with water," I said, moving food around on my plate.

"Well, then, *bon appetit!*" he said as he speared a tomato.

As hungry as I was, I forced myself to eat slowly, to drink plenty of water, and to skip the bread completely. I'd eat later on, after Nicholas was long gone.

"Do you mind if I call you Jennifer?"

"That is my name, so no, I don't mind." I knew I was being snarky. I didn't care. I couldn't help it.

He smirked. "I don't want this to be difficult between us."

I tilted my head. "And why would it be? I'll be gone in two months, then the villa is yours."

He took a long swig of wine, wiped his mouth with his napkin, and cleared his throat. His eyes turned more gray, it seemed.

"Jennifer, I'd like to buy you out of the remainder of your contract, with extra money for your trouble, of course."

My heart pounded within my chest wall. I set down my fork, placed both hands in my lap and dug my nails into the palms. It kept me from throwing food and utensils at his head. "No, thank you. I'm happy to stay."

He ran a hand through his hair and stared at a spot above my head for a long moment before speaking.

"It's just rather important that I move in as soon as possible. You'd be doing me a huge favor." He leaned forward, resting his forearms on the table. He gave me a look that I assumed he'd give a woman he wanted to take into his bed. "Jennifer? Would you help me out?" He let his bottom lip drop slightly.

I leaned forward, too, and pushed my plate to the left. "I can assure you that it's even *more* important that I stay here until my contract is up. On the twenty-ninth of July, I will vacate this lovely home, but not a day earlier. And if it's necessary, I'll consult with my attorney about the matter." My heart was beating furiously and I was afraid that if I stood up, I would faint to the floor. I honestly didn't know if I even had a case. I'd have to re-read my contract, and as soon as the British buffoon left, I'd call Bernie. Shit.

"Please excuse me," I said. "I'm feeling unwell." I pushed back from the table. *Please don't faint, please don't faint.*

Nicholas stood as I stood. "Jennifer, please let's talk about this."

"I can't." Before my voice broke, I ran from the room and pounded up the stairs. He could see himself out.

**

I stayed in my bedroom with the door closed and the shades drawn for the remainder of the afternoon. When I finally rose, I slipped out of the bedroom and padded barefoot down the hallway to the back window. His car was gone. I let out a long and ragged breath and went down the back stairs to the kitchen. Swallowing two aspirin with what was left of the San Pellegrino, I composed a text to Bernie. *He was here today. Nicholas. Call me when you can. xxx*

My phone rang a minute later.

"Bernie," I sighed into the phone.

"Oh, Jen. Honey, I'm sorry. Was he at least civil to you?"

"He sounds polite because he's British," I said, making her laugh. "He could tell me to burn in hell for all of eternity and it would sound civil."

"You're right. But he showed up without contacting you? He's not supposed to do that."

"Oh, Francesca knew. She'd set the table, even put out fresh flowers. And made lunch. Bernie, he wants to buy me out of my contract. He wants me to leave." Saying the words out loud made me shiver. Please don't let this be legal, I thought. I hadn't thought enough about what I would do when the end of July came. Where would I go? It was a topic I'd been avoiding. Nicholas was forcing me to think about it.

Bernadette paused before speaking. "What did you say?"

"I said no! He went on about it being very important that he get into the house as soon as possible. He even offered me extra money. Idiot. I wouldn't budge, though. I'm here until the twenty-ninth of July. He can't make me move. Right?" I crossed my fingers.

"No, he can't. And I'll call him. He can always get a short-term rental in Lugano. Maybe I'll suggest the hotel, drive some business to the kids. Jen, I'm really sorry."

"Thanks. I'm okay now. I just want him to leave me alone."

"Let me speak to him."

"Come visit. Please?"

"I will. I have a week of vacation next month. Always when the children get out of school. So I'll see you soon. But call — or text — anytime."

**

Bernie phoned me the next afternoon. I had just changed into my swimsuit and was ready to step into the pool when the phone rang. "I spoke with him earlier this morning."

"Tell me everything," I said. "Wait. Should I be sitting down? Do I need a glass of wine?"

She laughed. "It's okay. Sit if you want, drink if you want. I can wait."

"No, go on. I'm ready," I said.

"Well, I called him and re-introduced myself. He remembered me. And yes, he was very polite."

"Of course he was. It's that accent." I moved out of the sun and adjusted my chair to sit under the big umbrella.

"Yes."

"What is it? Bernie, is it awful news?" I steeled myself for the worst. Would I have to pack everything tonight and move into the hotel?

"No, it's fine. He understands. He will honor the contract and wait until you've moved out at the end of July."

"Really? No problems, then?" She paused before answering.

"None, Jen."

CHAPTER TWENTY-THREE

The wedding invitation for Donnalee and Rodney's wedding arrived in the mail. I took the oversized envelope outside, knowing what it was, and sat by the pool to open it. A cream-colored linen envelope the size of a notebook was sealed with lavender wax in the shape of a heart. I rolled my eyes. Here we go, I thought. Over the top Donnalee. But I had to smile — Donnalee was nothing if not predictable.

Inside the envelope, I found another envelope, and the invitation, and cards. I was invited to bring a guest, but I had no one to bring with me. The wedding reception was to be held aboard a boat, on the lake. That could be interesting, I thought. Once on board, there was no getting off until the party was over. That bit of information nearly made me respond with a 'So sorry, can't make it,' but I answered in the affirmative, added my name, only my name, and checked off the fish option.

**

The next day was rainy, all day. Whenever I walked on the Olive Trail in the rain, I always remembered the older man I'd run into months earlier, when I'd first arrived in Lugano. The widower, the man with raindrops on his long nose, who didn't care that he was soaked through, he was so bereft with grief.

I arrived back home wet and chilled, and changed into dry, warm clothes. I looked forward to being inside for the rest of the day, with a mug of hot tea and a good book. I left a note in the kitchen for Francesca, requesting her chicken soup and something sweet. Comfort food. There were oranges in a bowl on the kitchen counter and I carefully peeled and sectioned one, then laid the wedges on a plate to form a flower pattern.

I'd no sooner settled myself on the sofa, my bare feet tucked under a soft blue blanket, a steaming mug of chamomile tea on the table next to me, alongside my orange sections, when the front doorbell rang. Who was that? I wondered. I prayed it wasn't Donnalee. I'd replied to her wedding invitation. It wouldn't surprise me if she tried to fix me up with a date. We'd had casual contact since my disastrous dinner party, and while she smiled and fawned over my shoes or my hair or my lipstick color, I think we both knew that she and I would never be close friends.

I peeked out the narrow vertical window next to the door and saw a uniformed delivery man. I opened the door and he bent down to lift a glass vase off the ground.

It was possibly the biggest bouquet I'd ever seen.

"Attento! È molto pesante, signorina. Dove posso metterlo?"

I shook my head. "English? I'm sorry, I don't speak Italian." Still, I thought.

He grinned. "Sure, miss. I say it's very heavy, and where do I place it? The vase?"

"Oh! Yes, right here is fine. Thank you." He set the cut-glass vase on the marble-topped table at the foot of the staircase. "Grazie," I offered, my lame attempt at speaking his language.

"Prego!" He gave a slight nod, then hurried out the open door and jogged through the rain to his delivery van. I wanted to give him a tip, but he was gone.

What a bouquet! Orange and red lilies, hot pink Gerber daisies and miniature white roses, all surrounded by lush ferns. I plucked a small white envelope from within the greenery and pulled out a card.

'With sincerest apologies for my boorish behavior. Nicholas.'

I turned the card over and over in my hand. It would be easy to accept his apology. But I wasn't moving out early.

CHAPTER TWENTY-FOUR

The month of June brought a noticeable increase in tourists. The boats on the lake ferried hordes of people from restaurants to museums. With the lake-facing windows open, I could hear voices and laughter all day. From my bedroom balcony, I watched the boats glide across the lake's still water, but I had no inclination to join the crowds. The restaurants, cafés, and grottos were busy as well. Only the Olive Trail remained relatively quiet, save for intrepid hikers, Germans and other Swiss, who were far more accustomed to walking than the Americans and Brits. That was good for me. I kept to my morning ritual and walked the route, alone with my thoughts.

June also meant thinking about my future. I had less than eight weeks left at the villa. I'd pushed the thought away all through the winter and spring, but the visit from Nicholas had shaken me out of my self-inflicted stupor. Then the flowers arrived. I had no way to contact him to say thank you, even though I knew I needed to acknowledge his kind gesture. It was only right. Bernie would have his contact information, and she was due to arrive in Lugano soon to begin her vacation. Without Gerard, again.

Lucia invited me to dinner, apologizing for the last-minute text. I called the hotel to confirm with her directly.

"Jennifer, please don't be offended! Michel said it was fine to invite you with a text, although I don't agree."

"I'm not offended!" I really wasn't. Funny, how formal everything was while I was married to Jonathan. I knew protocol and knew how to behave like a proper senator's wife. But before I married him, while I was with Robbie, I would have texted an invitation, too. We never had a landline, and I didn't have any other way to communicate. I gave up a certain amount of freedom by becoming Mrs. Jonathan Logan, and I adapted to it well, but texting me to invite me to dinner? That's how I would have done it, too. "Really, thanks for the invitation. I'd be happy to join you. Has Bernadette arrived yet?"

"Her train comes at four o'clock."

"Oh, no car this time?" I recalled her telling me that she preferred trains to automobiles.

Lucia laughed into the phone. "She says that a true vacation means no driving. She hates to drive!"

"Yes, I remember. I also dislike driving. Perhaps

because we both drove so much in America." Although Bernie had lived in Switzerland for a long time, she was like me. In just a few short months, I didn't miss driving at all.

"Oh, I would love to drive more! And I thought all Americans liked driving. Doesn't everyone have a car?"

"Yes," I said with a laugh. "I guess Bernie and I are more Swiss than American."

"Yes, I suppose so. See you soon, Jennifer."

"*Ciao*, Lucia."

**

I had time to bathe and change my clothes. Checking the boat schedules, I noted that I could hop on the boat in Gandria at five and arrive in Lugano by five-thirty. I grabbed my purse, sunglasses, and keys, and closed the door behind me as I hurried down to the dock at Gandria, where a few dozen tourists waited. Some were sunburned, some were loud, all seemed very happy. It sounded like the United Nations around me. I listened to words and tried to figure out the language. Russian? Japanese? Definitely German. English, British English. I turned to see Nicholas speaking into his phone as his free hand raked his thick hair into spikes.

He was in Lugano, specifically in Gandria. Where

was his fancy car, I wondered. He was really lowering himself to ride the lake boat with the masses. I watched him as he continued his conversation, but I couldn't hear any of it once he paced away from me. Not that I wanted to eavesdrop, but I just hoped he wasn't complaining about the villa situation.

I still needed to thank him for the flowers. A note would have been easier. A text, even. And I had planned to ask Bernie for his address or email. Now it was almost certain he'd see me and I would have to thank him in person. A trickle of sweat crept down my back and I stepped out of the late afternoon sun into the cooler shade.

The boat pulled up to the dock with whooshes of water, and the crowd inched forward until a uniformed person who looked very important shooed them back. He made them stand to the right as four people made their way down a wooden ramp, then he removed a heavy chain that served as a barricade, as with a wave of his hand, beckoned the tourists aboard.

I stood close to the far edge of the crowd, as far away from Nicholas as I could. Once I was aboard the boat, I found a spot toward the bow on the starboard side and turned my face to the window, my straw hat pulled strategically across my left cheek. I was really looking forward to dinner at the hotel with my friends, and didn't need anything to stress me out before I arrived.

As the boat pulled away from Gandria, I dared to shift slightly, then a little more. I donned my sunglasses and ventured a look around the interior of the boat. It was his hair, golden in the sun, that was like a beacon. Nicholas stood outside against the railing and even from where I was seated, I could see the muscles and sinews in his bare forearms. A dusting of fine golden hair glinted in the sun. The breeze lifted his hair. As he turned and stood in profile, I felt something I hadn't felt in years, not since the early months with Jonathan, when every word, every smile, every touch was new. When compliments were sincere. When one look from him could turn my insides to butter.

Don't be ridiculous, I told myself. I removed my sunglasses and watched as Lugano grew closer.

"Pardon me. Jennifer?"

I'd just re-applied lipstick and was preparing to disembark. I wanted to wait while everyone else, including Nicholas, got off first. But I knew the voice immediately.

"Oh, hello." I stood. "What a surprise." I accepted his outstretched hand. His was cool and dry. I knew mine was not.

"I'm staying in Gandria for a bit," he said, slipping his phone back into his pocket. His mirrored sunglasses hid his eyes, which I remembered were a mix of green and gray. I didn't want to remember such details.

"*Prego*," the man in the uniform called to us. Everyone else had disembarked.

Nicholas gestured for me to go before him and I stepped carefully down the ramp. The dock at Lugano was festooned with colorful triangular flags, the kind I recalled seeing at car dealerships back home. There was Vivaldi playing somewhere, and an old man in a long white apron sold gelato from a white cart on wheels.

"Would you like one of those?" Nicholas's voice at my side was like honey in the sun. He inclined his head toward the gelato cart.

"Thank you, but no. I'm on my way to meet friends for dinner. They run the Hotel Walter." I pointed to the dominant yellow building across the street.

"Ah."

"Oh!" I tapped my fingertips against my temple. "Thank you for the flowers. I had no way to reach you. They're lovely, and they're still in full bloom."

Nicholas removed his sunglasses. There was a lot of green in his eyes, or maybe it was simply the reflection of the leaves on the tree above us. "I behaved badly. And I had no idea..." He trailed off, then touched my shoulder with a gentle hand. "I'm so sorry."

"You had no idea about what?" Without thinking, I took a step back, away from his touch.

"Bernadette, your rental agent? The woman I dealt with after I purchased the villa? She called me to let me know that your husband died recently, that's why you're here. I'm so very sorry."

"She told you." Dammit, Bernie.

He rubbed his thumb across his stubbly chin as his very green eyes looked into the distance, off toward Gandria. "Yes. I hope you're not upset. I think she wanted me to understand that...that it's important for you to be in the villa."

I felt a headache creeping in. "You know, I really have to go. Um, thanks again for the bouquet." As I turned away from him, I tripped on a cobblestone and pitched forward. Nicholas caught me around the waist just before my face hit the pavement.

"Whoa! That was close," he said, setting me back on my feet. "Those cobblestones are dangerous."

I was breathing hard. And so embarrassed. He must think I'm a klutz, a weepy, unhinged widow klutz.

"Another reason to say 'thank you,'" I mumbled. "I'll be more careful." But my feet were made of lead. I couldn't move.

"Would you allow me to walk you to the hotel, Jennifer?" When he said my name, it sounded so pretty. He made it sound like a song, one I wasn't sure I wanted to hear yet. He touched my elbow, then removed his hand and put it in his pocket. "Come with me. I won't let you stumble." We began walking along the lake, slowly. We passed an elderly couple sitting on a bench. A small black dog nestled contentedly at their feet. "Are you running late, or do you have time for a brief stroll?"

"Late? No, I don't think so." I glanced at my watch. Bernie's train had arrived; she'd be at the hotel by now. What would she think if she saw me strolling with the man I'd complained about days earlier?

"Good. Because I'm enjoying this." We walked past the hotel until we found an empty bench facing the lake. "Sit for a moment?"

I sat on the bench and he lowered himself close to me. Our thighs brushed, and I moved away an inch. What was happening? I lifted my face to a light breeze, hoping it would dry the tiny beads of sweat I felt forming at my hairline. He was attractive, yes, and it had been a long time since I'd felt anything like what I was feeling.

But I was nowhere near ready to allow those feelings in.

"That's Monte San Salvatore," I said, pointing to the hill in the distance. "I've promised myself that I'd take the funicular to the top before the end of my stay." My remaining weeks loomed now, and I felt an urgency to get to the top. "And there," I added, turning toward him, to point over his shoulder, "is Monte Brè. It looks pretty at night. The lights form a strand right up to the top, like a diamond necklace."

"Jennifer," he said, "if you ever want to talk, you know, about things...well, we speak the same language." He rolled his eyes. "Oh, that came out awful."

It wasn't awful. But I couldn't imagine the two of us chatting about my dead husband. I knew it was time for me to get to my friends. "I didn't know you were staying here. I guess I assumed you'd returned to England."

"No, my job is here, in Lugano. My employer is based in the UK, but we have branches everywhere." He laughed. "I've been relocated several times, but I'll be here for at least the next three years. It's why I bought the villa, and why I wanted to move in right away. But that would have displaced you, and it was inconsiderate on my part."

"I didn't realize. So you're staying in a hotel?"

"No, I found an apartment through a colleague. I can stay there until..."

"Until I'm gone."

"Until the end of July." He gave me a crooked smile. "No sooner."

"Oh dear, now I actually am late. I'm sorry, but I do need to go." I stood up, as did he. He stood very close to me and when I breathed in, I took the scent of him into my lungs. It rattled me.

"Can I trust you to cross the street by yourself?"

"Yes," I replied with a hearty laugh.

"And would you agree to have dinner with me sometime?"

I searched his eyes for a sign of joking, condescension, mocking, anything. I saw only sincerity.

"Sure." But even as I spoke that one-word answer, I wondered if I was ready. Dinner with Bernie was not the same as dinner with Nicholas — I was well aware of the difference. I wasn't searching for a new love. "But it's not a date, Nicholas. It's dinner."

"Yes, of course. Brilliant. I'll phone you, Jennifer. Enjoy your dinner."

"Bye."

"Good night." He stood in the same spot until I crossed the street and turned back to wave at him.

CHAPTER TWENTY-FIVE

In spite of my reluctance to allow Nicholas a place in my heart, and in spite of my knowledge that I had plenty of room in my heart to love again, there was a lightness in my step as I floated like a bubble into the hotel's dining room, where Lucia's son was placing glasses on the table at the back. With the hotel full, there was now a screen to divide the family's table from the rest of the dining room. Even as we ate at a table away from the guests, Lucia rarely sat as she kept watch over her diners and servers. On that lovely evening, the dining room was only about half full — I could understand, because there were plenty of options for dinner in Lugano — in outdoor cafés, in the simple tavern-like grottos situated along the lake's shore, even aboard the evening boats that offered dinner.

"Well, look at you, Jennifer!" Lucia exclaimed, leaving a table of two to greet me. "You're radiant!"

Was I? "Thanks for the invitation," I said, realizing just then that I hadn't brought anything for the hostess. My face grew warm with embarrassment but Lucia seemed not to notice. "Am I too early?"

"Not at all. Bernie is in the kitchen with our chef." She placed her hand alongside her mouth and, with a sidelong glance, added, "I'm worried he'll slice her!"

"Oh!" What does one say to *that*?

"One moment," she said and disappeared, just as the other children entered the dining room through their private residence door.

"*Ciao*, Jennifer!" Isabella chirped. She ran to throw her little arms around my thighs. I smoothed her curls.

"Jen." Bernadette emerged from the kitchen alone. "I swear, Lucia has hired the most thin-skinnned chef. I simply suggested that he add scallions to his dish and he freaked out! Good to see you." She kissed my left cheek, then my right, and then my left again. Three kisses, Swiss style. She stepped back and narrowed her eyes at me. "You've changed. What is it?"

"I haven't changed," I countered, taking her hand to lead her away from the table where the children had seated themselves. "Come here, I have to talk to you."

She followed me to stand by an empty table in front of one of the large floor-to-ceiling windows that looked out over the busy street. "What's up?"

"Did you tell Nicholas that I'm a widow? Is that why he sent me flowers?"

She pulled at her hair. "Well, I did mention it. After the way he showed up unexpectedly at the villa, upsetting you so much, I called him."

I sighed. "And?"

She looked exasperated. "And, I told him you'd been through some difficult months and he shouldn't be rude." She looked at me with questions in her eyes. "Why? What did I do wrong?"

"I saw him on the boat from Gandria this afternoon. We started talking. I thanked him for the flowers. He was much...kinder."

Bernie grinned. "Uh, that sounds *good*, Jen. And is that why you look so...glowy?"

"Well, wait," I interrupted, but I was likewise interrupted by Lucia calling us to dinner.

"Tutti a tavola."

"Come on, we'll catch up later," she said, pulling me away from the window.

**

Bernie and I strolled to the Bocc Bar after dinner, after I'd thanked Michel and Lucia and said good-night to the kids. The boys were sweet and Isabella was adorable, but it didn't give me pangs to birth any of my own. At thirty-four, I was very much aware of my own biological clock, but it hadn't bothered me at twenty-six when Jonathan told me he'd been 'neutered, snip snip.' Some people aren't meant to be parents. Many of those same people do it anyway. I knew it all too well.

"So," Bernie began, as she traced her fingertip along the rim of her glass. "Do you like him?"

I scowled. "I'm not sure. He was kind, as I said. The bouquet he had delivered was lovely. Huge. I don't know if he was trying to impress me..."

"Men do that, you know." She smirked and took a sip.

Words swam in my brain. "I didn't come here to meet someone, you know. It's only been a few months. And he knows I'm a recent widow." I stammered out one justification after another.

"Of course," she replied. "You ask yourself if your heart is large enough to accommodate more than one love. After Gary died, I didn't think there could ever be another. But I realized I still had love to offer."

"Yes, but..."

"But," Bernie guided me, "now you know that he's aware of your situation. Right?"

"He knows nothing. He knows my husband died, that's all he knows. He doesn't know anything about Jonathan, how old he was, nothing."

"Jen. What is it? What about your old life has you so rattled?" I watched her copper curls bounce around her head. "Listen," she said, "you know what I mean about Nicholas. I understand grief. You've told me that your marriage was difficult."

"It *was* difficult. But I loved my husband, especially at the end." I swallowed down the lump that had appeared in the middle of my throat. That lingering tinge of guilt. What could I have done differently? I'd downed my martini in record time and was nearly finished with my second. I would be a morbid companion if I wasn't careful. "I'm visited by memories constantly."

"Of course. And he'll always be with you, just as Gary is always in my heart." Bernie stared into her glass and I was reminded that second loves don't always work. She looked up at me and I noticed again the fine lines around her eyes. Laugh lines. Good for Bernie. "But Jen, you're young. And it's okay to love again. Your heart is big and there's room."

"I know." I bit my lower lip before saying what I'd been afraid to say out loud. "I think I love Jonathan more now that he's dead. It sounds absurd, I know. Perhaps

I'm idealizing our relationship." I knew that wasn't true — it was easy to remember his harsh words and ridicule, but I could just as easily recall his tenderness. "Sometimes it's hard for me to fathom how I can cry over the loss of Jonathan, and ten minutes later, smile because Nicholas said something charming. And though I would in no way use a word such as 'love' with him, I do *like* Nicholas. Well, more than I did the first time we met. But I'm only here for a few more weeks. Why start something now?" The reality of having to leave hit me hard and I felt a wave of nausea rumble through my gut.

"So for the next few weeks, why not enjoy yourself? Live *your* life! You're beautiful, far too beautiful to hide away in your villa."

Her words stung. Was that how she saw me, hiding away? I'd initially come to the villa to grieve in private. I'd fled the prying eyes of the media who didn't like me from the day Jonathan had brought me home as the second Mrs. Logan. I'd wanted to avoid any and all questions relating to his death. But what was my purpose in spending six months in Lugano? How would I have grown by the end of my stay? I didn't want my time at the villa to be a detached segment of my life.

"It's as if Jonathan is still here, you know? Not always, but when I looked at Nicholas, when he smiled at me, it was as if my husband was standing between us, keeping us apart. Keeping a safe distance between us."

"Did you enjoy spending time with him?"

"Yes," I whispered. We both fell silent.

Bernie traced her finger on the marble-topped table. "Jonathan. Did he have cancer? You never said, but I assumed."

The nausea hit me again, pushing bile up my throat. I swallowed it down with more vodka. "Yes. He was diagnosed just before Thanksgiving. It was pretty far gone by then." I hadn't talked to anyone about it, not even Nancy, my trusted assistant. Bernadette was now my closest friend. "He had postponed two colonoscopies; he said he didn't have time for the prep. By the time he saw his doctor, the cancer was at Stage IV, and had spread to the liver. He tried to return to Washington in early December, since there were only a couple of weeks before the Christmas break, but he had to return home within two days. He was adamant that no one know about it. His doctor advised him to begin chemotherapy and radiation immediately. Surgery was not an option at that point." I'd opened the dam, a tiny bit, but water was seeping through and pressure on the dam had increased.

"I'm so sorry. It went quickly, then."

A pang gripped my heart and I nodded.

"Jen?" Bernie laid her hand over mine.

"At times, he was the strongest man I ever knew," I whispered. "He never showed weakness, he never asked for help, and even when he was in so much pain, he could still smile at me."

"Did he have medicine for the pain?"

I looked up then and met her gaze. So gentle, so caring. Bernie cared, and I sensed that she could see right into my heart.

The sound of water rushed through my head. "He had a lot of medicine, yes. His doctor made sure of it." I bit my lip, hard. If I drew blood, I didn't care. "He'd had enough. Shortly after midnight on Christmas Eve, on Christmas morning, while I dozed in the next room, he took it all." The vise, like a belt cinched tight around my chest, broke free, and I took the deepest breath I could. I filled my lungs with air. Air as pure as the mountains and lakes of Switzerland. I filled my lungs again before speaking. "He had asked me to line up his meds, said he wanted to make sure he had everything he needed. His doctor was waiting in the kitchen, waiting for me to say goodbye, apparently. Jonathan begged me to get a good night's sleep in our bedroom. I'd been staying with him in the chair next to his bed, and that night, Christmas

Eve, he'd taken my hand and looked into my eyes and smiled and asked me if I would promise to sleep in our bed that night so that we could enjoy Christmas together."

"Jen..."

"He begged me. He said it would be a loving gesture if I would simply get one night's rest. He told me he couldn't have had a better wife. I'd never seen my husband cry until that night." I slumped in my chair, drained of all emotion.

Bernie moved her chair closer, and put her arm around me. I rested my head on her shoulder and nearly fell asleep right there in the Bocc Bar. I'd never known such exhaustion.

CHAPTER TWENTY-SIX

My hangover was gone. Bernadette had put me in a taxi, paid the driver, and she must have called Louie, because he was waiting when the cab dropped me off at the villa. He'd helped me up the stairs into my bedroom, and deposited me, fully clothed, on my bed. I slept until ten and, after two cups of strong coffee, one tall glass of cold water, and a croissant filled with peppery ham, I was back to feeling human.

Nicholas phoned early in the afternoon. "How are you?" he asked in his clipped accent.

"I'm fine, thanks." No need to recount the previous evening's festivities.

"I was thinking tonight might be a good evening for dinner. Are you free?"

As an eager hopefulness coursed through my body, I reined it back and offered a measured response. "Sure, why not?" I said. We both needed to eat. I wouldn't drink, though, at least no vodka. No vodka for a very long time.

He picked me up in his fancy black car, but drove to

the boat launch in Lugano and parked across the street. Instead of taking the big tourist boat, he'd commissioned a small motorboat just for us, a water taxi. He spoke in fluent Italian to the operator, then offered his hand as I climbed aboard. We sped across the lake to Campione d'Italia, the tiny enclave on the opposite shore.

"Are we in Switzerland or Italy?" I asked.

"We are in Italy! Surrounded by Switzerland."

The restaurant was rustic and delightful, situated against a sheer cliff that towered over the diners. Of course, I thought about avalanches and rocks falling, but Nicholas pointed out the heavy-duty nets that were installed above the restaurant. Afterward I tossed a few francs into the slot machines at the casino and quit after losing the equivalent of fifty dollars in less than ten minutes' time.

"Jennifer, why don't you stay on in Switzerland?" he said later, over a shared tiramisu.

His hair was golden in the candlelight of the restaurant. "I still have a few weeks left." I smiled.

"You know what I mean. The weeks will fly by. You'll start packing. I'm sure you're as aware as I am."

I was. The closer I got to the end of July, the more quickly the days seemed to pass. I'd been procrastinating about making a reservation for my flight back to the States, delaying the inevitable. But I didn't know how I could stay on, and I wouldn't hang around just because Nicholas Radcliffe suggested it.

**

Bernie and I had talked about the inevitable, too.

"Will you return to Rhode Island?" she'd asked.

"I don't know. I don't want to, there's nothing for me there except my mother, and she doesn't even recognize me." When Bernie asked me to explain, I simply said, "Lots of brain damage from lots of alcohol abuse." A sober calm permeated the silence. "Maybe I'll travel. I just can't seem to focus. I do wish I could stay," I'd confessed. "This feels more like home than home."

"And Nicholas?"

"Nicholas," I murmured. "No. Look, I like him. He took me to dinner and we laughed a lot. But I'm not going to pursue a relationship with him. Besides, why would I if I'm leaving the country?" Bernie gave me a curious look. "What?"

"Nothing," she said, tossing her head. "You trust me, don't you, Jen?"

"Of course I do. I trust you more than anyone else I

know. But for what?"

She patted my hand. "Don't book that flight just yet."

**

Donnalee and Rodney's wedding was in three days, on Saturday. When I had RSVP'd and indicated I'd be attending solo, I hadn't had anyone to bring with me, and I hated the idea of going alone. Now I had Nicholas as a friend, and I wanted him to go with me. The thought of spending hours on a boat at an event of Donnalee's creation was daunting enough. Having someone with me would help me get through it. I asked Nicholas if he'd accompany me and he was quick to accept.

I dialed the bride-to-be's number and listened to it ring.

"Donnalee, it's Jennifer Logan."

"Oh, Jennifer," she panted into the phone. "Are you not coming now?"

"No! No, I'll be there. And I apologize in advance for this question, but..."

"Oh God, what now? I can't handle any more changes."

Should I not ask? I didn't want to push her off the

edge of whatever pre-marital cliff she was dangling from. Then again, Donnalee was a drama queen. Everything was either a disaster or the most perfect occurrence ever. I plunged ahead.

"Since I responded to your invitation, I've met someone, and...would it be a terrible

inconvenience to you if I brought him to the wedding?" In my opinion, this was her chance to repay me for her rude behavior at my dinner party.

"Well, it *is* an inconvenience, Jennifer, I'm sure you know that. My guest list is a disaster." After taking a deep breath and exhaling audibly, she added, "For you, only for you. What does he want, fish or chicken?"

"Chicken for him. I already marked fish for myself. Thanks, Donnalee, I'm really looking forward to seeing you. Now, relax and enjoy the next few days. You're going to be a beautiful bride."

"Oh, Jen. I haven't eaten since last Wednesday. I can't relax. We have family flying in tomorrow morning, the hotel lost my parents' reservation, and Rodney has hives. I'm the only sane person right now. You can't even imagine."

I *could* imagine. That was why Jonathan and I got married in a simple ceremony in his living room, presided over by his friend the judge and attended by two couples he knew. I had no one except Kate, my former roommate, who stood up for me. But Donnalee didn't know that.

"I'll see you on Saturday."

"Don't you dare wear white," she said, and hung up before I could laugh.

I had to call Nicholas. For the 'inconvenience' I'd caused her, I'd write a big check.

**

The wedding was memorable. Yes, 'memorable' was the word I would use when I talked to Bernie. I took a few photos to show her, because she'd never believe it otherwise. Donnalee wore a Princess Diana knock-off wedding gown, complete with giant puffy sleeves and a ridiculous train. I was surprised she didn't arrive at the dock in a glass carriage. Rodney still had hives, and they were visible on the left side of his face. Donnalee's parents were demure and soft-spoken, and I was convinced they had adopted their daughter.

I recognized some of the guests from the dinner party I'd hosted months earlier. Only one of them, Milo, greeted me. The music was all from the early eighties — Michael Jackson and Blondie and Queen. Good dance music, I had to admit. Nicholas and I had a great time, goofing on the decor and the enormous cake, dancing to fabulous music, and I was glad he'd gone with me.

"I would never have had such fun if I'd come alone," I said to him toward the end of the evening. We stood outside at the rail as the boat made its lazy way back to Lugano. "Thanks for coming with me."

"It was brilliant!" he said. Beads of sweat clung to his forehead where he'd pushed his hair away. "It was as much fun as I could have had on a non-date date," he said with a wink.

**

Bernie telephoned me the Monday after the wedding. After listening to me ramble on about Donnalee's Diana-themed dress and over-the-top makeup, the decent food and very good music from a mediocre disc jockey, she finally interrupted me.

"Jen, stop! For a minute. I have news that's a whole lot more important than a recap of Donnalee the Diva Bride."

"Well, it had better be, for cutting off my captivating tale," I said with a laugh.

"I wish I could do this in person." Her voice broke at the end of her sentence.

"Bernie, what is it? Are you okay?"

She sniffled and made a soft intonation of sorrow. I could tell she'd been crying. "Yes, yes, I'm all right. Really. Gerard and I had a long talk this weekend, about everything." She paused. "We're splitting up." At my gasp, she continued. "It's okay. And it's been a long time coming, Jen. We've been living separate lives for months."

"But Bernie, I'm still so sorry."

"Yeah, me too. But you know me, the silver-lining seeker. I'll be all right. And there's more to my story, if you can believe it. Are you sitting down?"

I wasn't. I was standing in the middle of the living room, near the tall windows that looked out on the lake. My lake.

"I'm almost sixty, Jen. And my grandchildren are growing up so fast. I miss them when I'm here in Bern, and I miss Michael and Lucia, too. They're my family. So, I've decided to retire and move to Lugano."

I shrieked with glee. "That's fantastic news! Oh, dammit. By the time you relocate, I expect I'll be gone. But I'm still happy for you." This was her good news. I told myself to shut up and be happy for my friend.

"Thanks, I'm happy with the decision, too. Of course

my boss was anything but happy when I told her. She asked what she could do to get me to stay."

"She offered you more money?"

"She certainly did! But I told her that my mind was made up. And then I told her that I had a possible replacement for her." She paused. "Someone who might be able to assume my duties."

"What are you talking about?"

"Jennifer! I want you to interview for my job! Be the rental agent!"

I gripped the phone so hard my hand hurt. But I didn't want to drop the phone, because if I dropped the phone, the bubble might burst.

"Are you there?"

"Yes. Yes, yes. But...how...?"

"You can remain in Switzerland if you have a job. Sarah is willing to speak with you, on my recommendation."

Still clutching the phone, I walked to the window. I opened it and stepped out onto the small balcony. It was built more for decoration, but there was enough room to stand outside. I felt like I was flying over the lake, all the way up to the summit at Monte San Salvatore. I hadn't gone to the top yet, but now, maybe I could. Maybe I could stay. My stunned incredulity kept me from shouting.

"Is it legal, Bernie?"

"Yes, of course. Sarah wouldn't agree to it if it weren't. You know these Swiss! Now, you need to meet her for an interview. Can you come to Bern this week?"

"Sure! I could take the train today."

"Great. Gerard isn't here. He knew I wanted to pack my stuff alone. So come and stay here with me. We'll go together tomorrow and you can meet Sarah. Then we can return to Lugano together."

"Wait," I said. "Would I have to move to Bern for the job?" Bernie was moving to Lugano. I wouldn't know anyone.

"Not necessarily," Bernie said, and I could hear the grin in her voice. "Sarah needs someone based in Ticino. She never pushed me to relocate there because she knew Gerard couldn't with his job. But Ticino is the territory. You would have to get familiar with Locarno and Ascona as well as the other areas, but the bulk of your work would be in Lugano. *If* she hires you. I have to add that, Jen, because I can't make any guarantees."

"Wow." I stepped back inside and slumped to the sofa. "Just wow. Maybe I can stay."

"Text me with your train info. And I'll see you tonight."

CHAPTER TWENTY-SEVEN

I packed an overnight bag, adding the dress I'd worn to the wedding and my heeled sandals. There was a train in ninety minutes, so I called the taxi service and, while I waited, composed a message to Nicholas.

Heading to Bern (Bernie) tonight. Back on Thursday.

I stared at my phone for a minute. Why was I sending him a message? Nicholas and I didn't need to check in with each other. We weren't at that place, and I didn't necessarily want to be there. I deleted the message.

**

Bernie met my train and we walked together to her apartment.

"Are you okay?" I asked.

"The packing keeps me occupied," she said. "And I concentrate on seeing the kids again, this time for good. It helps." She offered a wan smile and unlocked the door to her place.

Bernadette and Gerard lived in a modest, well-furnished apartment. Small by American standards, the kitchen was something I'd expect in a Manhattan studio apartment. I wondered what she thought about my living, alone, in the big villa. She never offered an opinion, and I appreciated that. I had chosen the villa, over a one-bedroom apartment in the heart of Lugano, precisely because it was huge. I wanted space, and knowing it was only temporary was one of the reasons I had chosen it.

There were two large rolling suitcases near the entryway, and a cardboard box with handles that was half-filled with books.

"Is this everything?" I asked, glancing around the apartment. There were clocks and paintings and cut-glass bowls.

She nodded. "I don't want any of it," she said. She walked across the living room and touched the wall clock. "A wedding present from his parents." Then she took a couple of steps to her left and ran her finger down the frame of a painting. "We bought this on our honeymoon in Greece." With a pointed look, she added, "He can have it. I don't want any of this stuff, Jen. Everything I need, everything I want, is right there," she said, gesturing to the suitcases and the box. "It's a lot easier to leave it all behind."

"I understand. When I came here, I put our house up for rent, fully furnished. I didn't care about the knickknacks, either. I'd rather be free to move about."

"Exactly. So, let me show you your room."

**

I interviewed with the head of the rental agency the following morning at ten. Sarah, a stern-looking woman of about fifty, smiled when she shook my hand with a firm grip, but did not smile again for the duration of the interview. She asked me what other languages I could speak and I'm sure I saw a flicker of doubt on her face when I shook my head.

"At the present time, only English. I understand French better than I speak it, but I'm a quick study and I will try to learn both German and Italian," I promised. "And to improve on my French."

She asked me a question in French, and I had no idea what she had said. "I guess I need a lot of improvement." My knees shook under the desk.

"Yes. So, as of now you do not have fluency in any other language." She exchanged a look with Bernie, then continued. "Well, everyone speaks English, and your clients will be mostly British. Maybe a few Americans, although they tend to prefer tours by bus," she said.

If she accepted me, I would train with Bernie for three weeks, then I'd be on my own. If I was hired, it would be with a three-month probation period, after which time she could cancel our employment contract and I'd be leaving Switzerland. I nodded my understanding.

"What questions do you have for me?" Her manicured nails tapped on her computer keyboard and she looked not at me, but at her monitor.

Out of her sight, Bernie mimed driving a car. "Will I need a car for the job?" I asked.

"Yes. The trains are efficient, but you will need a car to get around faster. Usually you'll pick up the client, and many of the properties are up in the hills. When you have multiple stops in one day, it's absolutely essential." She cut her eyes to me. "Is that a problem?"

"No," I mumbled. I worried about it, though. I wasn't much of a driver, and I would much rather rely on Switzerland's excellent train network. But eventually I'd need a car.

"Anything else?" I saw her glance at her watch and I nudged Bernie.

"Sarah, you know I recommend Jennifer. In the past few months, I've learned a lot about her character, and I do believe she'd be a valuable asset to the agency. I remember you took a chance on me when I moved up here from Geneva, with only a teaching background."

Sarah pressed her lips together. "All right. Thank you both. I'll let you know, Jennifer." She pushed back from her desk and stood. I stood quickly and bumped the desk, nearly knocking over a delicate glass vase of daisies. Bernie grabbed it just in time. We shook hands and said goodbye, and I heard Sarah say to Bernie, "I'll call you later."

Once we were outside, I said, "I couldn't stop shaking. Do you think Sarah noticed?"

"I'm sure she didn't, Jen. Everyone is nervous in an interview. Don't worry about it, you did fine. Are you hungry?"

"No, my stomach's still in knots. Let's just walk."

And we did. From the rental agency's office near the train station, Bernie guided me past the Church of the Holy Ghost, to Bagpiper Fountain, to the main street in Old Town.

"If she hires me, I'll need a car," I said, breaking a comfortable silence between us.

"Eventually. But it's not something you need to stress about this minute. You'll get there, Jen. I'm not worried."

"What do you think?" I asked, stopping in front of a Thai restaurant. "Do you think she'll hire me?"

Bernadette leaned against the building. "Sarah trusts me, Jen. I recommended you because I believe you're capable of doing the job. She needs an agent who's situated in Ticino, and the fact that you're already there helps a lot. Now, you're an American, and in order for her to hire you, she'd have to enter into a working contract with you, meaning a commitment on her part. Either way, you understood what she said about the three-month probation period?"

"Yes. She could hire me, and let me go after three months if she doesn't want to keep me on."

"Right. Look, it buys you some time. I do think you'll like the work — you're well-suited to it. If it's what you want."

I wanted to find a place where I could begin a new chapter, and I couldn't see myself returning to Providence. Or Boston.

"I need to find an apartment." Bernie was going to live at the hotel. Of course that made sense, but secretly I'd hoped we might be roommates.

We found a tea-room and took the last table outside in the shade. After ordering coffee and a couple of gingerbread biscuits, our conversation turned to Nicholas.

"Maybe you won't need an apartment. There's room in the villa." She grinned as she stirred her coffee.

"No," I said. "I don't want that. I like being on my own."

"It's a big house. You don't have to share his bed...right away." She looked up at me. "Unless you already have?"

I smiled. "I haven't. We had a nice time at the wedding, but I've made it clear to him that I don't want to date him. If he wants to be friends, that's fine. I'm happy that we get along." At her raised eyebrows, I added, "Really!"

"You're going to tell him about the job when you get back?"

"Sure, if there's something to tell. If Sarah says no, there's no news to share, is there? I'll pack my things and figure out my next move. Maybe I could rent a place in France for a few months."

"One day at a time. Let's see how things go with Sarah first."

CHAPTER TWENTY-EIGHT

I felt that I owed Nicholas a dinner. I extended the invitation to Bernie and the kids, but they were busy at the hotel, which was fully booked, so they politely declined my invitation. I called Nicholas to invite him.

"I'd love to, Jennifer. How sweet of you."

I kept my voice light and breezy. "Well, you were kind to take me to dinner, and we had fun at the wedding. Besides, the place is yours soon enough, and I'm sure Francesca will be happy to cook for you." Light and breezy. "How about Saturday around six?"

"Brilliant. See you then."

Francesca seemed happy to have a long grocery list. Louie drove her and me to the market in town, and ran errands while we shopped. Together we selected artichokes, mushrooms, lemons, and cherries. Francesca suggested red mullet and umbrine, and since I wasn't familiar with either, I had to trust her. Arborio rice, salad rocket, and two bottles of white wine that Francesca deemed appropriate for the meal she was going to prepare.

I tried to explain to Francesca that Nicholas was just a friend, but I don't think she understood. Or maybe she didn't want to. Each time I mentioned his name, she turned coquettish and gave me looks I'd never seen from typically saturnine Francesca. As long as Nicholas understood, that was okay. I deliberately tried not to send him mixed signals, although the more time we spent alone together, the more it looked like we were a couple.

After we returned to the villa, I took a walk, and found myself in an unfamiliar area. As I had always walked the Olive Trail in the direction of Lugano, I hadn't explored the opposite way. After hiking uphill for some time, I came upon a cross that someone had stuck into the ground — two whittled branches, one upright, the other one nailed to it transversely. There were fist-sized rocks laid in a circle around it, and a photograph in a small plastic bag propped up at the foot of the cross with smaller rocks. I squatted down to peer at the photo. The woman in the picture was beautiful, like Sophia Loren. Long dark waves of hair surrounded high cheekbones and dark eyes. The woman in the photo was smiling — a big smile, lots of teeth, as if the person who took her picture had just said something to make her laugh out loud. She was full of life. I wondered who she was.

My husband was gone. It was, in the end, his choice not to undergo treatment for his disease, not to fight, not to linger as the cancer destroyed his cells. I knew he didn't want to suffer. I knew also that he didn't want me to bear witness to his decline. Was it right for him to do what he did? My upbringing said absolutely not. Some people would have said he was selfish, hostile. I couldn't judge his state of mind. My mother continued to subsist in a nursing home, at fifteen thousand dollars a month, and she didn't even recognize herself. But she was cared for, she was tended to by attentive nurses and aides. Even if she was cognizant enough to know that she didn't want to live anymore, she didn't have the ability to do anything about it. Perhaps Jonathan wanted to make the decision before it was out of his control. He wanted out on *his* terms, with me tucked safely away in my bed, unable to stop him. I loved my husband at the beginning of our marriage, and I loved him at the end. I would always love him.

And his presence would remain with me, the good and the bad. It wouldn't necessarily prevent me from falling in love again. But the process of letting go was tiring. I didn't have the energy to give to anyone else, at least not yet.

**

Nicholas arrived at the villa, at his villa, golden and leonine. Backlit by the rays of a late-afternoon summer sun, he bore a russet halo. I walked out the back door to meet him as he opened his car door.

He lifted himself out of his low car and I glanced behind him to his open convertible. There was a tan leather overnight bag on the passenger seat. Did he think I had invited him to spend the night with me? He seemed prepared for it, and if he was, he was presuming something that wasn't going to happen. I chose to ignore it.

He reached into the small area behind the driver's seat and pulled out two bunches of flowers, then followed me to the open back door.

Francesca hummed in the kitchen as she chopped vegetables at the big sink. At the sound of us entering her domain, she turned and smiled broadly at Nicholas. He presented her with a bouquet of brightly-colored flowers, similar to but smaller than the huge bouquet he'd had delivered to me weeks earlier.

"Oh, Nicola," she gushed. *"Mille grazie!"* She reached under the sink and found a glass vase, filled it with water from the tap and arranged her flowers with delighted hands. I would remind her to take them home when she left. Nicholas offered the other wrapped bouquet to me, and I bent my head to smell the intoxicating aroma of two dozen pink and white roses. He always goes big, I thought.

"Francesca, would you mind setting these in a vase, too? We can enjoy them in the dining room." I handed the bouquet to her and she actually grinned at me.

"We'll let you get back to working your magic," Nicholas crooned to his new best friend. She fluttered her hand at him and pushed her hair away from her eyes, then turned back to her chopping work, tapping her foot to a tune in her head. Nicholas gave me one of his crooked smiles.

"Should we have a drink by the pool?" I asked. "Francesca will call us when dinner is ready."

"Perfect." As he followed me out of the kitchen, he touched the small of my back, then traced his finger up my spine to my neck. A nervous little train followed his finger and I quickened my pace.

"I have gin and tonic for you. With limes."

"But of course," Nicholas said. He filled two tall glasses with ice, poured silvery gin, topped off with tonic water, and squeezed plenty of lime into each. "Cheers!" he said, clinking his glass against mine.

"To new friendships," I said, and he echoed back, "To new beginnings." I took a long drink and set my glass down. "So. I have news. Good news, I hope."

"Bernadette and Gerard are not divorcing after all?"

"Sadly, no. That marriage is over. But Bernie has decided to retire and move to Lugano permanently. She wants to be closer to her family."

Nicholas nodded. "That is good news. I thought perhaps your news had something to do with *you*, though, not Bernadette."

I took a long, deep breath. Perhaps I shouldn't say anything until I knew for sure. My staying in Lugano was important to me, not to us. There was no us, at least not at the time. I was keenly aware of the situation — the overnight bag in his car, just in case, his toast 'to new beginnings,' his finger trailing up my back. If I shared with him the news that I might be able to stay on, would he interpret it as a sign that I wanted to pursue a relationship with him?

"It does have to do with me. Bernadette recommended me for the job she has now, at the vacation rental agency. I went to Bern and met with her boss, who might be willing to hire me as an agent. I should know in a few days, but Bernie's endorsement means a lot. If I'm hired, I'll be able to stay, at least temporarily."

"Well, I'll be." He locked his gaze onto me. "I'd like that very much, Jennifer. Very much indeed." The corners of his mouth rose as he parted his lips and lowered them to mine. Without thinking, I pulled back, away from his kiss.

"What's going on?" He stepped back from me, adding distance.

"Look, we're just friends."

"Yes, you've been using that word a lot."

"Because that's all I can manage at this point."

"And yet you went to dinner with me. And invited me to accompany you to the wedding of your friend. And now dinner here. But you don't want to date." Was it angry blood rushing to his face?

I pressed my fingertips to my temples and controlled the rising tone of my voice. "I've tried to be clear. I've made an effort not to send you mixed signals. I like you, and I think we have fun together. But my husband hasn't even been gone for six months. And we know nothing about each other, Nicholas. I can't be intimate with you physically when I haven't a clue about who you are."

He dropped into a chair and crossed his ankle over his thigh. "So ask me then." His eyes were gray and steely.

I sighed. This wasn't going to go well. "Have you ever been married?"

"No. How did your husband die?"

"Oh, I see. I ask you, you ask me." He didn't change his expression and I thought about calling off dinner. "Cancer." If he wanted to give one-word answers, fine. I'd play his game.

Before I could lob another question at him, Francesca called to let us know that dinner was ready, and asked if we wanted to eat inside or out by the pool.

Nicholas stood and offered his hand to me. "I'm sorry. My bruised ego displayed my worst side. I did think that perhaps you were opening up to me. I was wrong, obviously. Let's eat inside, if that's alright." I took his outstretched hand and lifted myself from the chair, then let his hand go. "I'm fortunate to have a friend such as you, Jennifer."

CHAPTER TWENTY-NINE

Sarah hired me. I don't know if it was because of Bernadette, or because no one else had applied, or because she really did believe in me, but I was grateful for the opportunity and ready to prove to her that she had made a wise decision. Sarah reminded me that I was on a three-month probationary period, and that I had three weeks with Bernie as my teacher. After that, I'd be judged on my own.

By the third week of July, I had signed a new client.

A week later I moved out of the villa. Nicholas had offered to assist me on the twenty-ninth, a Saturday, but with Michel's suggestion, I managed to secure a moving company that brought a small truck to the villa on the twenty-eighth and packed my few belongings, then brought everything to my new, modest apartment in town, with no views of the lake. I left a note for Nicholas, wishing him *buona fortuna* in the villa. He had my number. After our dinner weeks earlier, we'd been more cautious around each other. I'd seen his temper flare and wasn't eager to see it again. We could be friends if he wanted — that was always my hope.

There were fireworks on the lake to celebrate Swiss National Day on the first of August. I joined Bernie and her family for a rooftop viewing at the hotel.

"And how does your Italian come along, Jennifer?" Lucia asked. First the first time that evening, she was seated, a glass of dark red wine in her delicate hand.

"I'm more mindful of words, but I could really use some lessons, I think," I said. "If you could recommend someone...?" I knew she was busy. As much as I would have liked to learn Italian from Lucia, she had no extra time to give me, and I knew it.

"Let me think about it, okay?" She stifled a yawn and set her glass down, untouched. "I think I should go to sleep. The morning will come soon. I wish you *buona notte*." She kissed my cheeks, then picked up her sleeping daughter and left the rooftop party.

**

As the days passed, I grew more confident in my job, and Bernie was ready to let me fly on my own. Nicholas was busy with work, and traveling a lot. We met for lunch in town one Sunday and he was restless, distracted. Our conversation was stilted, me asking mundane questions, him giving short answers. We smiled a lot at each other and I couldn't wait to be back in my little apartment, alone.

I knew I was not yet ready to love again. What I didn't know was whether it was fear, or guilt, or something else that was holding me back, but I did know that I was truly on my own and enjoying it. With Robbie and with Jonathan, I'd put up with, willingly, their idiosyncrasies, that which I found both endearing and infuriating. I adored Robbie's creative brilliance and resented that he wouldn't take on a part-time job to help us make ends meet. I fell for Jonathan partly because he was successful and secure, the opposite of what Robbie was at the time. I reveled in his attentiveness, but I loathed his arrogance, his condescension, and especially his deception. I had to trust my instincts that, when the time was right to let someone into my heart, I would be open to the opportunity. That time wasn't yet.

Sarah contacted me in the middle of August with a big assignment. "There are two separate clients, and both are interested in finding homes in Ascona. One is for next summer, and the other needs a rental for September and October. We have a few properties that I'd like you to show them. You can work with the family on Saturday and the business client on Sunday. Jennifer, I really wish you had a car," she clucked into the phone.

She was right. I knew I couldn't put off driving until the spring. My job depended on me being able to navigate the area, and that included all the areas surrounding Lugano.

"Can you get to Bern today? I'll have a car for you. Your driver's license will be fine. And I need you to pick up the keys to the homes as well as to the apartment we keep in Ascona. You can go there on Friday and stay the weekend. It will be easier than driving back and forth."

Bernie wouldn't be with me. My stomach muscles tightened with nausea. I took two long, slow breaths before responding.

"I'll be on the next train," I promised.

"Great. Let me know when you arrive," she said and clicked off.

I gathered up a few things and tossed them into a small bag, then called Bernie. My call went straight to voice mail. I left her a short message.

"Bernie, I've got two big assignments, both in Ascona, this weekend. I'm on my way to Bern now to meet Sarah and pick up keys and a *car*. Yes, a car – better stay off the roads! Oh, I do wish you could come with me. Call or text when you get this message." I ended the call and headed out.

By the time the train pulled into the Bern train station, it was late afternoon. I imagined Sarah waiting for me, so I hurried to the agency. She was the only person left in the office.

"Jennifer, sit down. Let's go through all of this. I want to be sure you don't have any questions. These are a couple of big clients, and you'll be on your own. Are you okay?"

I realized I was gulping air. "I'm fine. Just a little short of breath from running. I know you'd rather get out of here," I managed to say with a laugh.

She was serious. "No. I don't care how long it takes. I want to be certain that you're comfortable." She pushed an envelope across her desk. "Here are detailed descriptions of the three properties. Familiarize yourself with everything. I want you to be able to highlight all positive aspects of each villa. The keys are inside as well, and marked accordingly. Also, there's a single key — yes, that one. That's for the apartment in Ascona. You can go there tomorrow if you want. And when we leave here, I'll walk with you to the car. I assume you don't drive a standard transmission?" She raised her eyebrows almost to her hairline.

My heart dropped like a stone. "N-no, I don't. I never have."

"I didn't think so. You Americans like things easy." She smiled when she said it, but I didn't see any mirth in her eyes. "Don't worry, then. It's an automatic."

"Thanks. The clients, you said there's a family and a

businessman?"

"Yes," she murmured. "You'll see the family on Saturday. They're looking for a vacation villa, last two weeks of September, first two weeks of October. Three young kids. They want a view and a pool. All three properties have a pool, two have a good view. Now, the business client needs a place for next summer, June through August. Let me see, yes, he's teaching a summer course at a school there. It's just him, but he may want to do some entertaining." She leaned back in her chair. "Try to sign the family on Saturday. And let the gentleman know how quickly properties go for the summer — he's smart to look so early. Okay?"

I took a deep breath. "Okay." I glanced out her window. It was just about dark outside, and I'd have to drive from Bern to Lugano, at least a three-hour drive. Sarah must have read my mind.

"Jennifer, stay in Bern tonight if you're worried about driving in the dark."

I swallowed hard as I felt my neck grow warm. "I think I might. Just, you know, the first time."

When she smiled at me, her eyes were kind and sympathetic. "You're going to be fine, you know. I wouldn't have hired you if I didn't think so. Just pace yourself. The properties can almost sell themselves, but you'll bring an honesty and charm to them." She patted my hand. "Come on, I'll walk you to the car. You can leave it in the garage tonight."

I stayed in the Hotelbern, which was actually a Best Western property. Once I was situated in a large, clean room, I pulled out my phone and saw a missed call from Bernie. I punched in her number.

"Jen!" She laughed. "Are you in Bern now?"

"Yes. Oh, Bernie. I'm actually in a hotel. I can't drive back to Lugano tonight!" I told her all about the meeting and what my weekend looked like. "I'm terrified of doing this on my own. Driving, meeting the clients, selling the properties."

I sensed the slightest of pauses before she spoke. "You're going to be just fine. I have every confidence in you, Jen. I know the villas in Ascona, and you don't have to worry about them at all. The hardest part will be for the clients to choose. And as for the driving, just take your time. Set the GPS and follow the directions. If you get lost, you'll always find your way back."

"I wish you could be there with me!"

"No, this is your time now. And I'm headed to Fribourg this weekend to visit my friend Hanna. But you'll be fine. We'll catch up after you're back."

I couldn't tell if it was Bernie's subtle way of asking me not to contact her over the weekend. She'd be busy with her old friend. If I had any problems, I'd have to handle them myself.

"Sure. Listen, have a good weekend."

"You too, Jen. Try to enjoy Ascona while you're there. It's a beautiful place."

**

The drive from Bern to Lugano was about as gut-wrenching as I thought it would be. The car came equipped with a speaking GPS system, but as soon as a female voice began talking to me in German, I had to pull off the road and figure out how to change it to English. I listened to a male voice with an English accent and decided it reminded me too much of Nicholas, so I changed it again to a female voice.

There were tolls, and plenty of construction delays, especially around Olten and again in Airolo. And why did I have to drive so far north just to head south, I wondered. But I did it. A trip that normally would take about three hours took me five, but I was home. I parked the car in the underground garage, thankful that my apartment had its own parking space. I'd give myself plenty of time to get to Ascona, and I needed to do test runs of all the properties on Friday, in anticipation of my busy weekend days.

The following morning, after a quick breakfast, I drove along the A2, past farmland and the industrial areas of Bedano and Sigirino, through the roundabout, and headed toward Locarno. I drove around the top of Lake Maggiore and once I passed Locarno, I arrived in Ascona, an hour after I'd left Lugano. I parked the car and found the agency's apartment.

Ascona was charming. A wide pedestrian plaza stretched along the lake, and small boats tied up at moorings beckoned to tourists. And there were a lot of tourists. Every outside table was occupied. I closed my eyes and listened to the symphony of glasses clinking together, a stanza of some old Italian song sung in a lusty baritone, the distant rumble of a motorboat on the lake. I walked to the old town and found myself standing across from Santo Pietro e Paolo, a creamy yellow and white basilica with a tall gray bell tower, or *campanile*, next to it. A sign tacked to the entrance told me the church was closed. So, I walked back to the lake and found an empty seat at one of the outdoor cafés. I ordered coffee and opened the envelope that Sarah had given to me.

There were fact sheets on each of the properties, as well as a sheet-sized map indicating the locations. All seemed to be within a reasonable distance of the other. The family was due to arrive by train on Saturday morning and I would meet them at the station. They were Australian, and looking to rent for four weeks, the last half of September and the first half of October. I wanted so much to do well — as my first solo assignment, I knew a lot was riding on my performance. I had all day Friday to drive around to the villas and familiarize myself with the area.

My phone beeped with a message. It was Sarah with a text asking me to call her immediately. I gulped down my coffee, left money on the table, and signaled the waiter. Stepping away from the noise of the café, I walked down to the lake and found a bench under a tree. I dialed her number and waited.

"Are you in Ascona, Jennifer?" she shouted into the phone.

"I am. I arrived about an hour ago. The apartment is perfect."

"Good, good. Listen, your Sunday client has cancelled. He let me know that his company found a place for him, so he doesn't need a rental. Too bad, he was looking to rent for the entire summer."

"Oh. That is too bad. But the Australians are still arriving on Saturday?"

"Yes, as far as I know. I hope so. So spend all the

time you need with them, and let me know what they decide."

"I will, Sarah. Thanks." We hung up. I crossed my ankles and stared out at the glassy lake. It really was too bad the teacher had cancelled. That would have been a great rental. But now I didn't have to stay in Ascona through Sunday. Once I was done with the family on Saturday, I could drive back to Lugano.

CHAPTER THIRTY

Wendy and Graeme Percival, and their three very rambunctious children, liked the second house the best. It was enormous and modern, up in the hills with spectacular views of Lake Maggiore. Inside it was very white, and I made sure that Wendy and Graeme understood about the security deposit as their children ran screaming through the house.

With the papers signed and the deposit payment recorded, we shook hands and I let them know where they could pick up their key in three weeks' time.

"Ripper," Graeme boomed. "Well, missus, let's round up the hellions and have a plate. We've got a train to catch at four if we wanna be in Zermatt tonight. Good onya, Jennifer! We're right stoked about the place."

I assumed he was happy with everything by the grin on his big face. Wendy had run off in search of her children. Good luck to them, I thought. We'll likely get to keep that security deposit.

We all squeezed back into my car and I dropped them off by the lake. The Percivals headed off in search of a 'plate,' and I returned to the apartment. It was only mid-afternoon on Saturday, and I was free to remain in Ascona for the night if I wished. Bernie was away for the weekend. But why stay in a crowded town that would surely be noisy at night, especially when I didn't know anyone? As I drove away from Ascona, I was elated over my success. I had booked a major rental! It was cause for celebration. But my best friend was away for the weekend.

**

I neared Lugano and the traffic had increased. It was, after all, a warm Saturday. By late afternoon, folks were headed somewhere, either back home after a day in town, or coming into town for the evening. I spotted a parking space near the Hotel Walter and pulled in. After feeding money into the meter, I slipped out of the car and sprinted to the hotel's entrance. I couldn't wait to share my good news with Michel and Lucia. But as I climbed the steps to the dining room, it was clear that I'd picked a most inopportune time to visit. The dining room was completely full, and Lucia moved quickly from one table to another. I knew better than to bother her, and turned back to the stairs.

Donnalee and Rodney were on a delayed honeymoon — a couple of days earlier, I'd received a postcard that read 'We're in Prague and loving it! Next stop Vienna!' Good for them, I thought, as I manuevered the car back into the underground garage at my apartment building.

I checked my watch and realized I had just ten minutes before the market closed, but it was only a two-minute walk. I picked up nutty Gruyère cheese, a half baguette, and two lush tomatoes. A bottle of red wine and a small chocolate tart. If I had to celebrate alone, at least I'd enjoy myself.

Back at my apartment, I unpacked my items. I still felt the elation from my successful day and, on a whim, dialed Nicholas's number at the villa. I had to share my good news with someone, and though Nicholas was at the bottom of my list, I was sure he'd be happy for me. My desperate need for someone to congratulate me turned into a lesson in life.

"Hello?" The chirpy voice of a young woman, with a clipped British accent, had me thinking I must have dialed the wrong number. But I knew I hadn't.

"Um, I was calling for Nicholas Radcliffe. Is this the correct number?"

"It is! He's in the shower at the moment. Wait, I think I hear him. Hold on. Nicky? Babe? Can you come to the phone?"

Nicky? Babe? I didn't know who she was, but I didn't wait to find out. I disconnected the call and flung open the doors to my tiny balcony. Nicky babe!

It was true that we knew nothing about each other. It was also true that the distance between us had lengthened over the past few weeks. All I knew of Nicholas was that, according to him, he'd never been married. I had made it clear that I didn't want a relationship, so of course he would have moved on.

My phone rang. Nicholas. Shit. I let it go to voice mail. Sure, I was a coward. I didn't want to have to talk to him. It was a mistake to have phoned him, and it was only because I was needy for someone to give me positive feedback about my accomplishment.

It wasn't that I was shocked. Or disappointed. He had moved on, and I needed to let it go.

I couldn't see the lake from my balcony, but in the distance, a motorboat buzzed along the water. Bass notes from an amplified sound system emitted a muffled boom-boom-ba-boom. I listened for birds, but heard none.

Nicholas and I were not going to be friends. We had different interpretations of friendship. I viewed him as a dinner companion, a good conversationalist, someone well-read who could discuss a myriad of topics. At some point, I'd be ready to love again, and would want intimacy with a man. But I didn't know if Nicholas would be that man, or if he would even want the same thing. That our initial friendship hadn't turned romantic or sexual didn't bother me, but I knew that Nicholas felt rejected. He saw our relationship progressing in a way I couldn't envision, at least not for some time. That he needed something different than what I wanted was understandable.

I checked my phone for messages, but there were none. I opened the bottle of wine, sliced one of the tomatoes, some of the cheese, and tore off a hunk of bread. My celebratory dinner was served.

CHAPTER THIRTY-ONE

Bernie was enjoying her new life. I joked with her that she'd miss working, but I couldn't have been more wrong. My friend was ecstatic to be living with her family. We had a standing date on Wednesdays for supper together. It gave her a break from the hotel and I was able to tell her all about work.

"So, fill me in on your week," she said. "You always have more to share than I do. Not that I mind!" We were outside at the Grotto Teresa, across the lake from Gandria. If I stretched my neck, I could probably see the campanile of the villa, but I didn't try.

I told her about Ascona, and the big, noisy Australian family that rented the very expensive property overlooking Lake Maggiore. I told her about the businessman who cancelled for Sunday. I told her all about driving. And finally, I told her about Nicholas and the woman who had answered his phone.

"Whoa! You saved the best for last. Or was that the worst?"

I scooped up some polenta with my fork. "Well, I was surprised. I shouldn't have been. He wanted a relationship, I didn't. He moved on."

"Are you two still friends?"

I chewed for a long time; I didn't know the answer to her question. "I don't know. I don't think so."

"Gary and I were friends first," Bernie said.

"You were twenty years old. It's different."

"I guess," she shrugged. "What do *you* want?"

"I want to be successful at my new job. I want Sarah to keep me on. I want to feel comfortable driving. I want to speak Italian."

"Nicholas isn't a part of any of that." It was a statement, not a question, and I nodded in agreement. "Did he think your friendship was more than a friendship?"

"I'm sure he hoped it would be more. The times we spent together, I tried to be clear that we weren't dating, but I think he hoped, yes."

"I hoped, too. You made a cute couple."

I brushed a stray strand of hair from my face. "I'm just not ready. You know, probably better than anyone, Bernie, how complicated grief can be. Leaving Providence and relocating to Lugano hasn't filled the void in my heart."

"Letting go is one of the hardest things," Bernie said. "And by that, I don't mean forgetting him. I mean that you find compassion for him, for you. I remember, right after Gary died, I felt as though I was walking around in a fog. It kept me from functioning, and I kept waiting for it to lift. But it didn't. And I thought that perhaps every day would be filled with that fog, that my new normal would be to exist within days where grief was a heavy blanket sewn to my shoulders. Then one day, and I can't tell you when it was, but one day I noticed the sun was out. It wasn't the first sunny day, but it was the first day since Gary had died that I *noticed* it. His kids flew in, to Switzerland. We spread his ashes in a special place, and Justin, Gary's son, said something funny. And I laughed, Jen, I genuinely laughed. That night I slept. I was grateful for the rest. I still cried, and I still cry. That's how grief can be — you hate it, but sometimes you welcome it."

"I can't affix blame to Jonathan for what he did, because I don't know what I would do given the exact same circumstances. I do wish he had trusted in me, but I understand why he chose not to."

"You have so much potential, Jennifer." She patted my hand, and I was ready to lighten the conversation.

"And I'm loving my job."

"And you're driving!"

"Yeah. Well, Sarah wanted that to happen sooner rather than later. I'm going to use the Toyota for now. I'm comfortable with it. And they'll give me an allowance for expenses." Bernie grinned. "The August vacation rentals are set in place for the most part, but there's always a last-minute request for a villa or apartment. Well, you know that."

Bernie pushed her clean plate to the side and said 'yes' when the waitress asked if we wanted coffee. I declined, hoping for a decent night's sleep, and asked for herbal tea instead.

"So, it's been three weeks since I signed the divorce papers," Bernie said, stirring milk into her coffee. "I felt that the split was amicable, that Gerard was fine, and there wasn't any acrimony. Then yesterday I learned he's moved a young woman into our house. Sorry, *his* house. She's thirty, younger than Michael. Unbelievable." She tossed her spoon on the table.

Her anger wasn't lost on me. It was probably how Virginia felt when she learned that Jonathan had remarried. Bernie didn't make the connection, apparently, and I asked instead where she bought her shoes.

**

In September, my mother died from a massive

stroke. I flew home to give her a proper funeral and burial, and said a silent prayer of thanks that her ordeal was over. She hadn't had a good life, partly due to her own poor choices. Poor choices that set her down a steep path of decline, one from which she was unable to climb up and out. When I was about fourteen, she had said to me, "Because you're beautiful, life will be good. You'll see."

She was wrong. Life wasn't good because of my looks. Poverty is poverty, and no matter what I looked like, I was still hungry at night. I wore clothes from Goodwill or the Salvation Army. I washed my hair with bar soap and missed dances, football games, and friends. Life could have gone in an entirely different direction for me.

I may have been blessed with good genes, and many people told me I was beautiful, but beautiful wasn't about bone structure and long legs. I don't think my mother ever understood why I hated the name Farrah. And my looks had nothing to do with my life. My life was awful and lonely at times, and no amount of beauty would change the fact that we were poor, or that I was ridiculed in school. Or that I worked hard for everything I ever achieved. Beauty may have caught the eye of a middle-aged senator, but I wasn't under any fairy-tale princess delusions that being with him would change who I was. My circumstances changed, and I had more money, but there was a price, certainly. I stayed with Jonathan because I had vowed to. And I loved him, even when I didn't particularly like him. In the end, when he gave up the fight, I let him go.

**

I spent two weeks in Providence. While I was there, I met Joe Greeley for lunch. His firm had relocated across town, to a bigger space, leasing two floors of an old, renovated factory that used to manufacture silverware. He took me on a tour, and I loved the exposed brick walls. It reminded me of my old loft apartment in Boston. Joe's corner office was expansive and sunny, and before I said goodbye to him, I told him to watch for a surprise delivery.

His brown eyes twinkled and he opened his desk drawer. "I still have some of the Swiss chocolate you sent me. No one else knows about it, that's why there's still half a bar left."

"This is something different," I replied. "Just be patient." Once outside, I called the gallery on Newbury Street and recognized the breathy, sing-song voice of Charmaine. I introduced myself and asked if she'd ship the painting, the big painting of the match factory where I'd lived with Robbie, to Joe Greeley's office. It would be a perfect fit and it would finally have a home.

**

By November, I was a permanent employee of the agency and booking villa rentals for the following spring and summer months. I was better at driving, and grateful that the winters in Ticino were relatively mild. There wouldn't be a lot of driving up into the hills, not during the winter. I went to Bern twice a month to meet with Sarah, who commended my job performance. She hadn't been wrong about me, she said, and I smiled. Even my language was improving. Lucia had never gotten back to me about Italian lessons, and I didn't want to bother her by asking again, so I took the initiative on my own.

A few weeks before Christmas, I spotted a notice on a public bulletin board in the market:

Hello! Do you desire to speak Italian? I will help you. I am Carlo Cesana. His email address was written at the bottom of the notice.

I sent him a message and included my telephone number, and when he called me the following day, we had a lovely conversation. He had a quiet, gentle voice that was hypnotic and soothing. I asked him how long he had been teaching Italian.

"Yes, I am new to the teaching of Italian, but I am speaking Italian all of my life. Do you agree that I am qualified?"

I laughed. "You make a good point, Carlo. Yes, you are qualified."

"You see, miss, I am a widower, and my children, they tell me that I should be busy. I should find something to occupy my days."

We agreed to meet on Thursday evening at six at the pizzeria across from the boat dock. I arrived a few minutes early and looked around the café but didn't see an older single man. So I sat down and ordered a San Pellegrino.

At five minutes past six, a man approached my table. "Are you Jennifer Logan?" he asked. I looked up at the tall man and nodded. He took a seat across from me and I realized I was staring.

"You look familiar, Carlo," I said. Where had I seen him before?

"You do also."

"I've been living here since January, almost a year now."

A waiter approached, and Carlo ordered coffee. We spoke about Lugano, and he used Italian words whenever possible.

"I am adding *zucchero* to my coffee," he said, as he

stirred sugar into his cup.

"I'm sorry about your wife," I said. "*Mi dispiace.* When did she die?"

"Two days before Christmas," he replied. "*Due giorni prima di Natale.* Losing her was like losing my skin."

I kept staring at him. His long, narrow nose. "My husband died on Christmas Day," I said. "*Niente è per sempre.*" I spoke aloud the first phrase I had learned in Italian, so many months ago. "Nothing is forever." And as the words left my lips, I realized, and Carlo must have realized, too. He reached out and touched his finger to my cheek, which was as wet as it had been that day on the Olive Trail, when we first encountered each other. Carlo, who was consumed with grief that rainy day.

"It's you," I whispered. "I kept returning to the Olive Trail, hoping to see you."

He smiled at me then, his cheeks furrowed by strong feeling. "I couldn't return for many months," he said. "*Molti mesi.* My Viviana was always there."

"And now?" I asked. "*E adesso?*"

"Now I return every day," he said.

"Why? *Perché?*"

"Because she is always there," he said. "She is in the sun, in the sky, in the olives on the trees. Viviana is there, walking with me."

"*Grazie*, Carlo," I whispered, brushing at my cheeks. "*Mille grazie.* I look forward to learning from you."

Carlo placed his large hand over mine. "*La speranza mi da vita*," he said.

I shook my head. "*Speranza.*"

"Hope."

"Hope," I repeated.

"Mi da vita."

"*Vita*," I said. "Life? Hope is life?"

He patted my hand and smiled. "Hope gives me life. You are a good student, Jennifer."

I smiled back, my heart full of hope.

Acknowledgments

Many thanks to those who provided me with advice, feedback, and corrections throughout the process of writing this novel. Writing is a solitary experience, but there are many involved in the pre-publication stage, and I am grateful for them.

I am grateful to Michelle Vezina for technical advice, Barbara Green-Studer for inspiration over lunch in Fribourg, Pauline Wiles for critique and feedback, Brea Brown for being Brea Brown, Lottie Nevin for the exquisite cover art, and Amy Buser and Carol Wise for the cover design. I am a proud member of the Association of Rhode Island Authors.

Very special thanks to Fabiola Abbet-Dreyer for fixing all the Italian words and phrases. *Mille grazie!*

And, as always, my husband Jim is my biggest fan, my sounding board, my best friend. It's because of him that I can continue to do what I love so much.

Also by Martha Reynolds

Chocolate for Breakfast

Chocolate Fondue

Bittersweet Chocolate

Bits of Broken Glass

Best Seller

A Jingle Valley ~~*Wedding*~~

A Winding Stream

93299644R00186

Made in the USA
Columbia, SC
12 April 2018